PATH

OF THE

DEAD

PATH

OF THE

DEAD

MARK EDWARD LANGLEY

**BLACK
STONE**
PUBLISHING

Copyright © 2018 by Mark Edward Langley
Published in 2018 by Blackstone Publishing
Cover and book design by Djamika Smith

Printed in the United States of America

First edition: 2018
ISBN 978-1-5385-0759-9
Fiction / Mystery & Detective / General

1 3 5 7 9 10 8 6 4 2

CIP data for this book is available
from the Library of Congress

Blackstone Publishing
31 Mistletoe Rd.
Ashland, OR 97520

www.BlackstonePublishing.com

For my wife, Barbara; my daughter, Erica; and my mother and father, Polly and Jack, who always told me to keep going and never give up on my dream. I wish they were still here to see it come true.

CHAPTER ONE

The body of sixteen-year-old Renée Braun lay weak and warm, cradled by the moss and leaf litter of the forest floor. The severe drought that plagued the New Mexican landscape over the summer had given way to a welcome fall rain. The tall Douglas firs that stood around them were already beginning to turn gray in the falling rain, on their way to black. They began to weep softly as a mild breeze swayed the branches that had been soaking since early morning, turning limber again.

The forest had stood quietly by, final witness to the muffled cries and pleadings that had reverberated in the moist morning air. The girl's eyes, now wide with the realization that her life was coming to an end, heightened the sensation he felt coursing through his veins. Her fading whimpers were no match for the drowning well of blood that had already spilled into her lungs and now rose like a swelling tide in her throat. Flecks of scarlet began to stipple her face as she tried to grasp hold of her last fleeting breath, just before her eyes went still.

He watched in eager anticipation as the tide of blood swelled from her mouth and ran down both sides of her face to brighten the damp earth. Now the only sounds in the falling rain were the repetitive calls from a cast of falcons, carried on the mountain breeze from somewhere off in the distance. He reached out a hand and gently brushed away a few strands of brunette hair that had gathered across her forehead. *How beautiful you look*, he thought, *and how blessed am I that you have been chosen for me like all the others.*

On the morning that was to be the last in her adolescent life, Renée Braun had dressed herself in a thin white sweater over a pastel pink blouse, carefully paired with her new white denim shorts—shorts that had tantalized his imagination from the moment he saw her standing by the calm, smooth lake. His eyes had been drawn quickly to the frayed edges that caressed the tops of her creamy thighs before disappearing between them. And to the pair of simple white Crewcuts sneakers that adorned her perfect little feet—an unconscious afterthought of spontaneous teenage flare.

He replayed in his mind the cries that had begged him to stop, to let her go, whimpering that she wouldn't tell anyone if he would just let her go. But he had not stopped, and he could not let her go, because there was no way to stop the events that had already been set in motion. For this little temptress had to pay in the same way as all the others. She had to be made to see that she could not play with the emotions of men without suffering the consequences.

As he pulled the blade of his hunting knife from her body for the last time, he found himself on his knees, straddling her waist and tilting his head from side to side, admiring the mosaic of blood and flesh and clothing. He marveled at the images of blurred makeup and smeared lips that still managed to shimmer from the cinnamon lip gloss he had tasted as she fought his initial violation. He slipped his tongue out between his lips, like a reptile tasting the air, and savored the lingering flavor that remained. His eyes then wandered to the blackened rivulets of mascara that had drizzled down her face in jagged lines as she bore each downward plunge into her abdomen. Each thrust going deeper and ripping its way through already torn flesh and severed bone, until he had felt the tip of the double-edged blade bury itself in the earth beneath her.

His lungs filled with a kind of drunken satisfaction as he lifted the hem of the thin white sweater and slowly wiped her blood from his blade. He laid the knife on the ground beside him. Then he unbuckled his belt. Now she could be his. Now she wouldn't fight.

CHAPTER TWO

The clock on the docking station atop the nightstand declared "8:10 a.m." in black numerals backlit by a pale sea of incandescent blue. Arthur Nakai slipped out of bed and padded across the handwoven rug that covered the cold hardwood floor. For the past few months he had tried to be as quiet as possible in the morning. Sleeping late was a luxury that Sharon had just begun to enjoy, and he wasn't going to be the one to ruin it.

He showered quickly and was toweling off when something made him pause briefly and study himself in the oak-framed oval mirror above the washstand. He saw his father's strong jaw and proud nose and his mother's gentle eyes gleaming from above her high cheekbones. His damp black hair felt good brushing his clean skin. His shoulders were still broad and strong, and his chest and abdominal muscles where still where they should be after forty-five years of life. In fact, the only noticeable signs of encroaching middle age so far were the doughy love handles that now clung to his flanks, just above the belt line, like two well-formed links of smoked sausage.

He took a deep breath and let it out. *Forty-five isn't really a bad age to be,* he told himself. He was still fit and healthy, and the only things he had noticed, aside from the sausages, were the subtle changes that had begun to creep over his face. The faint wrinkles around his mouth and the corners of his mother's eyes, for instance. He grinned to himself, wedged his chin between thumb and fingers, and moved his head from side to side, then nodded approvingly to the image in the mirror before slapping the bathroom light off and padding back to the bedroom, smelling of sandalwood soap.

Pausing at its emptiness, the first thing he noticed was that their bed was now vacant and the sheets carelessly tossed. The second thing he noticed was the tempting aroma of breakfast seducing him. With the empty bed now explained, he pulled on a fading pair of jeans from behind the small door in the middle of his dark wood dresser, put on a red long-sleeved shirt from the closet, and covered it with a black leather vest that he took from the chair of Sharon's vanity. He was sitting on the end of their bed, tugging on one of his worn square-toed Justin ropers, when Sharon floated in wearing nothing more than one of his red-and-black flannel shirts and carrying a fresh mug of coffee.

"You know," he said, "there's something extremely sexy about a woman wearing only a man's shirt in the morning." He took the mug from her hands and savored the aroma, then the taste, and then the warmth in his throat.

Sharon smiled. "And what makes you think this is all I have on?"

"Because I saw you wearing nothing last night, and my ever

so observant mind can always put two and two together and end up with four."

Behind her smile, Arthur noticed something clouding her mind. He took another slug of coffee and gave her back the mug, pulled on his other boot, and stood. Sharon handed him back the mug.

"What's wrong?" he asked.

"I just had some trouble sleeping last night, that's all," she said. "I kept thinking about our life." Sharon looked down at her hands, loosely intertwined in front of her, before returning her gaze to her husband. "I was thinking that it might be the right time to try again."

Arthur sipped his coffee and swallowed. "Really?"

"Yes. It's taken me a long time to get to this point, and I want us to try again."

The possibility of children was something he had forced himself not to contemplate since the day it happened. He had always found other ways to occupy his mind, some other way of pushing it back into the darkness where, he knew, it would always be lurking. But now that past was falling over the edge of his mind with all the weight and the roar of Niagara Falls. What if it happened again? Was she ready to put herself through the same torment and devastation if it did? Could she survive it? Arthur exhaled. Could he?

Sharon bowed her head slightly, dark eyes rising to look at him from under her brow. "Don't you want to try again?"

Arthur smiled halfheartedly, shaking off the past. Her morning look of bare legs, flannel shirt, and shimmering ebony hair had captivated his mind. "I'm always up for trying," he joked.

"This isn't funny," Sharon replied, slapping his arm playfully. "You'd make a great father. I think we should try again. I mean, it's been two years …" She let the words hang in the air.

"I know it has," he said. "I count the days, too, sometimes." He took her hand gently in his. "It's just that we've never even gone into the room we locked after it happened. And besides, you're rarely home anymore, and I'm out galloping around the desert most every day. Kids take a lot of work. I just don't know that we're up for that kind of responsibility quite yet."

Sharon sighed as if from the weight of her thoughts. "So, it bothers you that my work keeps us apart."

Arthur said nothing as he led her out of the bedroom and down the stairs to the kitchen, where Sharon had already decorated the table with a plateful of pancakes stacked under a steam-lined plastic lid. Two pans, one of eggs, the other bacon, simmered on the stove, while two frosted glasses of orange juice and a stainless-steel carafe of brewed coffee waited on the table. After shifting the eggs and bacon onto their plates, they sat. All this time had given Arthur a chance to piece together his thoughts.

"That's not what I meant," he said. "I knew before we got married how important your career was to you, and I was okay with that. I just wanted us to be together and build a life. But look, if you're serious about having kids, maybe you should start eating twin ears of corn so we can make it twins."

Sharon grinned wryly as she pushed the eggs around on her plate. "Smart-ass. The doctor told us back then what caused it." She shook her head slowly with regret. "I should have been more careful."

Arthur just sat listening, remembering what the doctor had

said about the lambs and the Q fever and the infection's role in what happened. But no matter how many times he replayed the events, the thought that perhaps it *was* her fault had always found a way to creep back into his mind. What if she *had* put her career before her family? Was this how Kokopelli, the fertility god, had chosen to punish them? He pulled himself out of his dark well of thought, cut a wedge of pancakes, and ate it to give himself time to regroup. "What made you think of this now?"

Sharon looked at him over her juice glass and took a drink, then set the glass down and swallowed. "I guess I've just been so busy pouring myself into work, I never thought about what we've actually been missing." A smile of lost possibilities crossed her face. "He would already be talking now. You know, they say a two-year-old has a vocabulary of about seventy-five words?"

Arthur didn't answer. He knew she wasn't looking for one. Sometimes saying nothing was the best reply.

Sharon sniffled as her eyes grew moist. Suddenly, her face lit up and she smiled broadly from across the table. "You would have been telling him all the stories your father told you."

Arthur allowed himself the thought of doing all those things as he watched her move her eggs around on her plate in a stalling dance. He had the distinct feeling the other shoe was about to drop.

"I also think we've grown apart in some ways," Sharon said.

And there it was. The shoe hadn't simply fallen off; it had come flying at him. Arthur took a breath and let it out. He felt the quicksand in the pit of his stomach, and the dry tickle in the depth of his throat.

Sharon went on. "Sometimes we don't even see each other for days. And we hardly ever eat dinner together anymore." She waved her fork absently. "And you always sleep on your side of the bed now. You used to lie next to me and lay your arm over me and hold me." There was a short pause. "You haven't even done that in a long time. I guess I don't excite you anymore." She paused again. "Or maybe you blame me?"

Arthur tossed his fork onto his cooling eggs and heard it rattle on the plate. "I do not blame you! And of course, I'm attracted to you—you're my wife!"

"Really?" she countered. "Then why don't you act like it? I used to love all the little things you would do for me, but they're not enough anymore. I need to feel you next to me, but you never are. I need to know your warmth is there, but it never is."

Arthur sat at the other end of the table, sifting through his vocabulary. When one said the wrong thing at a time like this, the argument only escalated. He sipped some coffee, hoping it would loosen the constriction he still felt in his throat, but it didn't. "I'm just not sure if trying again is right for us now."

Sharon looked at her plate, stabbed a piece of pancake, and bit out the words, "I'm just trying to get us back to where we were before!"

Arthur thought very carefully about the next words that would come out of his mouth. Over the years, he had begun to understand her attitudes and their subtle complexity. He changed the subject to a less fraught path. "How are things going at the station?"

Sharon shook her head at the futility of talking with men. "They're fine," she said flatly. "I just need to change my life."

"There must be something going on," Arthur prodded. "You've only been back to work for six months."

Sharon ate in silence for a few moments. "It's just that as journalists, we're taught to separate ourselves from the story, to look at it as if we were simply a spectator. I find it harder to do that anymore, because there are always some stories that just linger in the back of your mind, only reaching out every now and then to tug at your subconscious, like a small child pulling on its mother's dress for attention. Stories like the Christa McDonald murder."

Arthur gave her a blank look.

"Men!" she said. "You all have the retention of a kitchen strainer. She's the woman who was murdered down around Silver City three years ago. She'd been working in the US Forest Service office for about six months when they found her dead in her apartment."

Arthur acknowledged that he remembered, then picked up his juice glass and drained it before picking up his plate and depositing them in the sink. He went back for Sharon's plate, along with his coffee mug, and rinsed them.

Sharon shook her head sadly. "She was stabbed to death in her bedroom. They believe her killer was there long enough afterward to wipe the place clean and take a shower after first positioning her body on her bed like she was flying."

Arthur searched for something to say, but that train of thought had already derailed. He remembered reading in the *Albuquerque Journal* about the murdered woman: good family background, graduated from Princeton, a bright future ahead of her. He also remembered reading that she had been found partially clothed and stabbed many times, the coroner stating that she had also been sexually assaulted after her death.

"Whoever did it left behind no DNA," Sharon continued.

"Not even a fingerprint or a strand of hair. The autopsy found evidence of a spermicide, so it's believed he used a condom—a condom that was never found at the scene, by the way, which means he was very methodical. And the fact that no hair follicles but her own were found on her body led the authorities to believe that the killer had probably shaved himself clean."

"From head to toe?" Arthur said.

"Head to toe," Sharon repeated. "And nothing was under her fingernails, either. It was like she never even struggled."

"Maybe she knew her killer?" Arthur said. "Or maybe he met her somewhere and they ended up going back to her place."

Sharon shrugged. "Maybe he took her by surprise, and she never had a chance. We'll never know, though. The detectives pulled all the unsolved murders from the past ten years and found nine more resembling hers, in different parts of Arizona and New Mexico. No one had ever put them together before. They're sure they can classify it as serial—kind of like the Chester Turner case in South LA."

Arthur remembered reading about it. Turner had been charged with killing ten women, including one who was six and a half months pregnant, in the 1980s and '90s. Christa McDonald's killer had been connected to at least ten murders in the past twelve years.

"He hides among us, he kills, and then he hides again," Arthur said, glancing at the regulator clock ticking away on the wall. "Shouldn't you be getting ready?"

Sharon glanced at the clock. "I have plenty of time," she said. "My overnight's already packed, and I wasn't planning on taking off from Farmington till eleven. Before you know it, I'll be landing in Belen covering the newest renovations at the Harvey House."

"The *Fred* Harvey House?" Arthur asked. "As in Judy Garland and the Atchison, Topeka, and Santa Fe?"

She smiled. Arthur liked it when she did. It always wrapped itself around him like a warm blanket.

"It's just a fluff piece," Sharon remarked, "but it's good for tourism and it's actually pretty fascinating. You know it's been around since 1910 …" Her mood seemed to shift suddenly, and she looked up at him from her chair as she began to unbutton the red-and-black flannel shirt. "I have to shower," she said, lightly biting her perfect lower lip. "Join me?"

Before he could answer, she stood and gave a slight shrug, and the unbuttoned shirt dropped to the floor. Arthur stood mesmerized. The morning sunlight slanting through the window behind him bathed her body in gold as she stepped up to him.

"I've already had a shower," Arthur said, mustering all the self-control he could to withstand this surprise attack. "And besides, Billy's already grooming the horses for today."

Sharon pressed herself into his body. "Billy Yazzie can just keep right on grooming," she said. "He won't miss you."

Arthur felt her fingers walking their way up his back, the dense fullness of her breasts pressing more solidly into his chest, and her pelvis conveying the rest. She stood on her tiptoes and softly kissed his mouth.

"Well," he added, "I do have that tour group coming at eleven o'clock."

"You're making it awfully hard for me, aren't you?" Sharon said, smiling.

Arthur smiled and pressed against her. "Actually, you're the one making it hard."

CHAPTER THREE

Sharon soared over the ten-foot chain-link fence surrounding the Alexander Municipal Airport in Belen, New Mexico, a little after one in the afternoon. The fence had been erected to keep curious animals, including any mischievous two-legged ones, from disrupting air traffic on runway 21 at the small airport, which, from fourteen thousand feet, resembled nothing more than a slivered laceration on the sandy landscape.

The Piper's landing was simple and straightforward for an aircraft of its size. Anything larger trying to navigate the field would have a pretty unnerving time of it. The electrohydraulic landing gear locked into place upon approach, and she soon felt the jolt and heard the chirp of rubber as the tires met the tarmac. The Saratoga PA-32R taxied toward a cluster of small planes parked near a Quonset hangar proclaiming SKYDIVE NEW MEXICO in ten-foot block letters. There, anyone wishing to experience the exhilaration of near death could shell out anywhere from ninety-five to two hundred fifty dollars for the thrill of pushing their luck. Sharon cut the power to the air-cooled Lycoming engine and listened to the familiar sputter as the Hartzell propeller spun to a stop.

She had left the Four Corners Regional Airport in Farmington that morning with mixed emotions. It had been a long time since they made love like newlyweds, since she felt his fingertips caressing her body, his lips kissing her throat, and his strong body covering hers. But she couldn't get the thought out of her mind that it had also been an automatic reaction to their argument. Had they both simply resorted to the only way they could still experience a connection after all this time?

Sailing on the upper-level winds, she had tucked away her thoughts enough to enjoy the solitude of studying New Mexico's deeply cut and textured surface. How the mountains wrinkled their way up from the vast plain, and the brown-and-ochre desert gave way to green forests; how the wandering lines of blacktop ran like varicose blood vessels across the land. When she was flying, she saw no boundaries and no counties, no fences of any kind. The land was as open and free as it had been in the centuries before the Europeans arrived and began carving things up for themselves.

She had decided not to program the GPS, but use the highways instead. Her flight plan had taken her along New Mexico 371, past Chaco Canyon, whose massive D-shaped remains passed slowly beneath her port window as she continued south to Crownpoint. She cruised over Hosta Butte at a comfortable 177 knots, then dipped her wing and banked southwestward on the winds off Mount Powel so she could connect with Interstate 40 at Thoreau. From there, it was easy to follow I-40 around the veined terrain of Blue Water Lake and the playa at Milan, which always reminded her of a giant stingray.

Pressing a hidden compartment, she removed a pair of aviators from their nest and slipped them on as other small towns rolled beneath the belly of the Saratoga. She floated over Laguna Pueblo and skirted the sprawling urban expanse that was Albuquerque. After lining up with Interstate 25, she headed south over Isleta Pueblo, toward her date with Mr. Harvey's House.

During the final leg of her journey, their conversation over breakfast replayed in her head. Had Arthur truly wanted to move forward, or was he just telling her what she wanted to hear? He certainly hadn't shown the spark she hoped to see when she put the question to him. He had lost a lot that day, too, and perhaps, as with her, not a day had gone by that he didn't think about it. But also, like her, he had managed to push it away and build a wall around it too high for it to climb over. Perhaps, she ventured further, he had locked it away somewhere just as she had done, deep inside the vault of her mind, where she would never find herself walking except on those dark days when the pain and loss consumed her.

Sharon turned her head briefly to look out the side window and wiped away a tear. After regaining her composure, she let her thoughts continue. That morning, the past had been ripped from the vault and thrown over the wall, where they would be forced to deal with it. She had thought that confronting the past would somehow free them to live for the future. But his reaction had shown her that the division between them, which had begun slowly at first, had quietly grown into an abyss too great to bridge.

It had started when little things began to creep into their daily life. They had begun to spend more time apart—not only because of work, but while at home, too. The horses seemed to require more of Arthur's attention, while she just lay in bed watching television, reading, sleeping, or awake and staring at the ceiling, trapped in her own thoughts. She had also begun to snap at him for things that never bothered her before. Innocuous things such as not replacing the paper towels before they were gone, not keeping fresh bottles of water in the refrigerator, not reading her mind and having the pot ready and boiling on the stove whenever she wanted hot tea.

She remembered being a basket case for most of the first year, while Arthur tried to walk on eggshells, tiptoeing around in fear of triggering one of her emotional avalanches. Nothing he could do or say was done right or said correctly. And whatever he had done right was always grounds for confrontation because it wasn't done the way *she* had always done it. She shook her head, wondering how he had even managed to stay around. Other men would have simply cut and run. Maybe he still would if he got the chance.

Sharon climbed out of the cockpit and onto the wing of the Saratoga as the mild weather of a new month brought the cool of October against her face. Shutting the forward cabin door, she carefully made her way down the sloping wing—a feat she had long ago realized was not easily accomplished in Michael Kors pumps, which was why she had taken a few minutes to change into a pair of neon walking shoes before leaving the Mesa. The rubbery soles of the pink-and-green shoes made it easier to descend the wing and absorb the ankle shock of hopping down onto the tarmac. She set down her overnight bag and went through the necessary procedure of securing the aircraft. Then she stood and smoothed out her tailored tan slacks and tugged at the end of her matching single-button jacket to look fresh and presentable.

The temperature hovered in the low seventies, and the mild breeze that roamed freely across the west mesa of the Albuquerque Basin filled the air with the mixed scents of aviation fuel and catclaw blossoms. Since Sharon last visited the airport, it had tried to move into the new century. She remembered reading in an aviation journal about the addition of a pilot's lounge with such unheard-of amenities as updated restrooms, showers, internet access, a conference room, and a kitchenette for those looking to take a break from whatever travels they found themselves on. Her black hair shimmered in the morning sun as she watched the KZRV news van pull up and stop.

Oscar Hirada waved and pushed open the passenger door. Sharon climbed in and tossed her overnight bag in the back. "Right on time," Oscar said. "I was hoping to at least have time for a nap before you plopped down in that thing you call an airplane."

"Hey, hey!" Sharon replied. "Don't be knocking my bird."

Oscar had dressed in his usual blue jeans, white Nikes, and Carlos Santana concert T-shirt from Las Vegas. His thick black hair was raked back over his head, and his mustache had been artfully groomed to droop past the corners of his wide mouth. To top off the look, he wore the wraparound sunglasses that *he said* made him look like Danny Trejo. Sharon just grinned.

"What?" Oscar said.

"Nothing," she replied, inwardly rolling her eyes as Oscar put the van in gear. "You know how to get to the Harvey House, right?" She took a compact from her purse, popped it open, and began applying makeup with a small round pad while trying to balance her reflection in the two-inch mirror.

"What, you think I'm unprepared for this journey?"

Sharon glanced over her left shoulder with an amused grin. "I seem to remember someone who said they knew the way to Bandera Volcano and somehow we ended up in the Valley of Fires."

Oscar mumbled something in Spanish, and the van lurched away. Sharon laughed and finished doctoring her face with the puff, closed the compact, and returned it to its assigned pocket in her purse.

On the way from the airport into town, Sharon noticed that some of the storefronts had changed names since her last visit to New Mexico's Bethlehem. A sudden realization washed over her that change was inevitable and could not be diverted or postponed. She wondered, what with change being such a constant, if she were to become pregnant from this morning's lovemaking, would it be a change for the better or for the worse? *Could Arthur have been right about us not having the time?* She hated second-guessing herself and was busy settling the whole train of thought snugly into a corner of her mind when she saw the rotating sign of the Wagon Wheel restaurant looming high above South Main Street.

"Pull in there, will you?" Sharon motioned with her chin. "I have to pee."

Four minutes later, Sharon emerged from the restaurant and

stood briefly in the bright sunlight until she located the KZRV news van. She walked across the parking lot, expecting to see Oscar behind the wheel with his seat leaned back, listening to *Santana Live*, but he must have had to answer his own call.

Sharon took a moment to pull her Blackberry from its storage pocket in her purse and check the time. Arthur would be in his element about now, sitting tall on his horse, leading a group of tourists on a trail ride. Some European or Japanese tourist yearning to be John Wayne had no doubt gotten him to dress them in Old West garb, while others would be content to fill their cell phones with images from the trail in New Mexico. Arthur had often remarked that he never felt more at home than when he was on a horse, without a road or building in sight. She could see it every day and wondered whether she would ever find that kind of contentment.

She tucked the phone back in its pocket, looped her purse over the passenger-side mirror, and slipped off her blazer. Draping it over her left arm, she retrieved her purse from the mirror and yanked open the van's swing-away door. She froze.

"You look even tastier in person."

CHAPTER FOUR

Arthur held a slack rein, leaning back in the saddle while the chestnut stallion descended the narrow dry wash. He redistributed his weight and sat straight as the horse crossed the sandy bottom, then leaned forward as it surged up the far bank. In three strong strides, it pounded up through the silt and pebbles to solid footing above. Arthur wheeled the chestnut around to face his small group and said, "Cross at the same spot, but let your horses pick their way down and up."

His group today consisted of a middle-aged German couple with choppy accents, a younger couple from Australia with suntanned faces and blond hair, and an almost elegant dark-haired woman in her mid to late forties from Concord, New Hampshire. When they had filed up the worn path out of the arroyo, Arthur turned his horse to the north and studied his afternoon shadow on the ground. Then, glancing toward the sky, he pretended to figure out their direction using the sun. Tourists loved that sort of thing. It supported their belief that Native

Americans could never get lost as long as they could follow the sun's path across Father Sky. Arthur never had the heart to tell them this particular old Indian's secret of marking the trails with subtle piles of stones so you always knew where you were.

In fact, the only thing the position of the sun had told him was that their six-hour ride would soon be coming to an end. Part of him was glad. But another part was a little wistful because he hadn't talked them into doing a pack ride and camping out for the night. He grinned to himself. That was always fun, helping them imagine the kinds of creatures that prowled the high desert night.

"Is that a coyote?" the New Hampshire woman asked, pointing to an animal striding between clumps of buckhorn and yucca. Her face was soft, but her mannerisms were that of a strong woman who didn't need a man to bring balance or meaning to her life.

"His name is Ak'is," Arthur said. "He's been following us since we left."

"I never noticed him before," the middle-aged German remarked. His looks reminded Arthur of the actor Gert Fröbe. He had paid extra to be decked out in the Hoss Cartwright hat with the tall domed crown, calf-length oilskin duster, bandanna, and chaps. Arthur had already taken his picture four times. Meanwhile, his wife had given him the impression that she was on this adventure only because her husband had wanted it and couldn't wait to be done with it all and back in the world of roofs and walls and paved surfaces and cars.

"He's pretty good at keeping his distance," Arthur explained. "Likes to be on his own."

"Is he some kind of dog, then?" the Aussie woman asked, shading her eyes with her hand.

"He's a wolf-dog: Siberian husky/timber wolf mix."

"I've heard they don't make good pets," the Aussie husband said. His eyes were hidden behind a pair of black Ray-Bans. Arthur wondered why he hadn't given them to his wife.

"That depends," Arthur said. "They'll generally do right by you when given enough love and freedom." He watched the creature's long trotting strides. "We have an understanding."

"Why did you name him *A Kiss*?" the New Hampshire woman asked.

"*Ak'is*," Arthur corrected. "It's a Navajo word meaning 'friend.' I found him as a pup at a shelter in Albuquerque. He needed a home; I needed a friend. That was six years ago."

Arthur slipped the strap of his canteen from around his saddle horn, unscrewed the top, and let it dangle from its small chain against the blanket-covered sides. He drank a mouthful and reminded his guests to stay hydrated. "Don't chug-a-lug it, though. Just a swallow at a time." He didn't need anyone throwing up on the horses or the tack.

The trail he had chosen took them in a wide arching horseshoe pattern through Arthur's part of northwestern New Mexico. He had handled the usual tourist questions with ease, trying to teach them a little about the Navajo way of life, and a respect for the land that most people had long forgotten. Now his guests were twenty minutes away from their vehicles, and he was the same distance from a comfortable chair and a cold beer.

Arthur swung the big chestnut around and gave a few whoops like a bloodthirsty raiding party. Tourists seemed to like that, too. It echoed off the cliff strata and reverberated across the open air, like a fleeting ghost that quickly diminished into silence. Now galloping at a strong pace, Arthur smiled between whoops. When he looked back, he noticed that two of the three women were losing stride. He slowed the big chestnut stud to a canter to let them catch up, then rode casually with them the rest of the way.

Arthur's mind tipped back to a morning conversation with Sharon a few weeks before. He remembered her pouring coffee, setting the carafe down, and saying, *"I just think I'm done with this job. It's bled me so much I can't bleed anymore."*

He remembered getting up and rinsing their dishes in the sink.

"I wish I could be like you," she had said. *"I wish I could just leave it all behind and not think about all the awful things going on in the world right now."* She sighed. *"Sometimes, being a journalist is like looking at the world through a filthy window. Every day, I go to work wondering what kind of cruelty humankind has inflicted on itself the night before."*

He remembered his mind working to figure out where this was coming from, then deciding to venture a guess. Arthur Nakai, Navajo shrink. *"I think, after years of developing a thick skin against what you were reporting, you find yourself questioning your own objectivity."* He grinned inwardly at the memory.

Sharon had watched the steam rising from her coffee. *"Maybe,"* she'd said. *"Do you ever regret leaving the Shadow Wolves? I mean, they were such a large part of your life for so many years. And you had that friend, right? The one who got shot."*

Arthur nodded. *"Abraham Fasthorse."*

Sharon smiled. *"That's him."* She paused. *"Don't you ever miss it?"*

Arthur had rested his backside against the kitchen counter, both hands gripping the edge lightly, and thought briefly about her question. *"Not really,"* he finally had said.

After three tours in the marines, he had spent the next twelve years of his life searching 2.8 million acres of Tohono O'odham desert for drug smugglers and UDAs. Some of the Shadow Wolves had even been shipped to Uzbekistan to teach the locals how to cut sign and track down their own smugglers. Most days in that job, he just left the house hoping to come home with the same number of holes he went to work with.

He remembered snorting a laugh and saying to Sharon, *"When they dissolved US Customs and dumped us in with the Border Patrol is when the bureaucracy kicked in. Under the guise of 'Homeland Security,' they confined us to seven-square-mile patrol areas and hamstrung us to the point where we couldn't be as effective as before. It's only improved slightly since then."*

As they topped the small rise at the end of the trail, Arthur noticed the arctic-white Chevrolet Suburban of Jake Bilagody parked alongside his ranch house. The sunlight glinted sharply off the light bar that stretched across its pale roof. The Navajo Nation Police Department of District Two in Shiprock had acquired three new vehicles that year, and Jake, being captain, had claimed one to replace his Ford Expedition that had seen better days.

His contentment with the new rig's stock appearance had faded quickly, however—so much so that after only a month, he had driven it to a four-wheel-drive shop in Farmington for a suspension lift and bigger, more aggressive tires that better adapted to the changing terrain of the area. All in the name of apprehending felons, of course. Arthur grinned and punched his heels into the chestnut's dark flanks. The big horse responded by bursting into a gallop toward the corral. The other horses quickly followed its lead, their hooves digging into the fine sandy loam and kicking up clods behind them.

Captain Jake Bilagody of the Navajo Nation Police relaxed on the side porch of Arthur's home, watching the riders come into view. His uniform shirt was clean and starched, just as it had been for the past twenty-five years of active service, and his pressed trouser legs had the same razor-sharp creases as always. His imposing frame filled the porch with a presence that seemed to pulsate from him like echo waves on a radar screen. Arthur sometimes wondered what it must feel like to be on the losing end of a confrontation with such a commanding figure.

Jake had tilted a rustic straw-seat chair back and taken up his usual position, with his polished boots resting on the wooden porch rail, as he sipped one of Arthur's ice-cold Santa Fe Nut Brown Ales. He looked on as Arthur led his guests to the corral and had them dismount for group pictures, taken with their phones. As the big German shrugged out of his duster and unbuckled the heavy leather chaps, Arthur took a moment to shake hands with each of them and thank them for spending the day with him, and for the liberal gratuities they were pressing on him.

Billy Yazzie had already begun unsaddling Arthur's horse as the guests walked carefully toward the parking area, some of them massaging tender backsides. Billy shook his head and grinned. Arthur helped him unsaddle the remaining horses in the corral.

Once the bridles were off, saddles racked, and blankets properly stored, he reflected on how smoothly the day had gone. Billy began the task of making sure the horses had enough water and feed as Arthur looped the circle of rope over the gatepost and headed across the hard-packed open ground to the house. The tourists drove away, leaving a small cloud of dust in their wake and waving as they passed. Arthur smiled politely and waved back as he stepped up onto the side porch.

"Who'd you have today?" Jake asked, finishing his last swig of Santa Fe Nut Brown.

"Two Germans, two Aussies, and a woman from New Hampshire who thought Ak'is was a coyote."

Jake removed his hat and wiped the barely damp bottle across his forehead, then rocked his chair forward.

Arthur noticed. "What's the matter, Jake, beer flat?"

Jake grinned halfheartedly. "Let's go inside, huh? Get outta this glare."

"Sure," Arthur said. "I need to wash down the dust anyway."

They walked together in silence along the back porch to the kitchen door and went inside. Arthur let the screen door slap the jamb behind them. As Jake pulled a chair away from the kitchen table and sat, Arthur pulled open the refrigerator door and grabbed a beer from the spill-safe plastic shelf. He held up another, but Jake declined, saying he was on duty and shouldn't even have had the first one. Arthur twisted the cap off and sat across from his friend, apologizing for the dishes stacked in the sink. Jake waved him off, reminding Arthur that he himself was now a bachelor again and was fully aware of how dirty dishes could multiply.

Arthur grinned sympathetically, aware that the mention of Jake's new single status was not an open invitation to discuss the recent past. After twenty-five years of marriage, Jake and Nizhoni Bilagody had finally agreed that what had bonded them together in the beginning was now gone. He remembered Jake sitting in that very chair nine months ago, telling him about the night he had simply looked across the dinner table at his wife and thought to himself that she would never again be the woman he married. *"That time is gone,"* he had said, *"never to return."* Then he added somberly, *"Some things you just know."* There had been too many changes in them both, too many things that turned their daily life together into a struggle, and their love had quietly, gradually faded until they were just two people living in the same house. No more than friends, no longer lovers. *"You know what love is?"* Jake had asked him. *"Love is a myth. A myth kept alive by greeting-card companies, candymakers, and songwriters. It begins as a strong fire but burns out over time."* He had noticed Arthur watching him as he lamented, then shrugged and warned Arthur with a wagging finger, *"Don't let the fire you two started with turn to ashes. Trust me on this. Once the flame of love goes out, you can no longer breathe life back into it. It is gone forever."*

Arthur let those remembered words sink in for a moment. "So … what did you drive your shiny new vehicle all the way out here for?"

Bilagody stopped playing with his bottle.

"There was a murder in the Cibola this morning," Jake said. "A sixteen-year-old white girl from Michigan, named Renée Braun. Chaves County Medical Examiner says she was killed with what appears to be a hunting knife—multiple stab wounds." Jake paused. "He also said there was evidence that her killer raped her after she was dead." The Navajo cop shifted in his chair and muttered, "Sick fuck. Anyway, the feds are going on the assumption this killing may be linked to other murders with the same MO over the last fifteen years, because of the way her body was laid out."

Arthur took a swig of beer. "Laid out how?"

"Her legs were straight and crossed at the ankles, while her arms were swung above her head and just out to the side, elbows slightly bent, like she was flying. Like a bird, you know?"

"Or an angel going to heaven," Arthur said.

Jake paused to consider that and then added, "But that's the telltale. The feds never released any info about how the other women's bodies were laid out, so it can't be a copycat. Must be the same guy. Their big break came this time when they discovered the killer had left behind some fingerprints along with some well-deposited DNA."

"What kind of DNA?" Arthur asked, twisting the bottle in his fingers.

"Medical examiner found semen inside the girl's body, as well as saliva mixed with the girl's blood on her vaginal entry. The killer has never left any evidence before, which means either this killing was unplanned or he was rushed for some reason. That's why the FBI isn't so quick to say anything to the press just yet concerning the girl's body. Their guy has never been this sloppy, so there's a slim chance it might not be the same person."

Arthur took another swig of beer and said a prayer quietly to himself for the girl in his head. "So why come to me? Feds need me to track him?"

Jake took off his hat and placed it on its crown on the table, then ran a big hand over his black hair to the back of his neck. "Arthur ... Bill Blackhorn of the Belen Police Department telephoned me about an hour ago. A car that was reported stolen from a campground in the Cibola was later discovered in a restaurant parking lot in Belen." He took a deep breath and let it out. "He also told me that some witnesses put a KZRV news van in that same parking lot a few hours before the car was discovered. The station has tried to contact the van but couldn't get a response. And neither Sharon nor her cameraman are answering their cell phones. They both go right to voice mail."

Arthur's hand tightened around the damp brown bottle. Jake's eyes darted around the kitchen before returning once again to Arthur's. "Some State boys found the news van abandoned at a construction site in Polvadera. One male was found in the back, strangled with coax cable."

Arthur's tone was flat. "Oscar."

Jake nodded, "Yeah."

"What about Sharon?"

"We don't know. Forensics went over the van and matched some of the fingerprints found on the steering wheel to ones that were found on the Braun girl's body."

"They can do that?" Arthur said.

Jake nodded. "There is a very small window and a special light source has to be used with film and whatnot, but it can be done." He paused. "Anyway, the Federal database came back with a name: Leonard Kanesewah. A Chiricahua Apache from Arizona, with a record since he was a teenager. The feds think he stole another car in Polvadera and is heading for Mexico with

Sharon as his ticket to ride. They found her purse and cell phone in the van." Jake rubbed his leathery chin. "They're considering him armed and dangerous, and now they've added kidnapping charges, so a BOLO has been issued across the four-state area and his picture will be on every newscast."

Arthur's mind worked quickly. "What kind of car is he driving?"

"Look, now, I know what you're thinking," Jake countered with that familiar wagging finger. "I don't need you out there playing Charles Bronson."

"That's because nobody took your wife," Arthur interrupted. "All I want to know is what kind of car he's driving."

"Just let the feds handle this," Jake pleaded. "The minute they have anything solid, I'll pass it on. You just need to sit tight and let them do their job."

"Bullshit!" Arthur leaned forward in his chair. "Some lunatic has my wife, and you expect me to just sit here on my ass doing nothing?"

"I'm telling you to stay put for your own good," Jake insisted.

"And I'm telling you, no, I don't believe I will," Arthur said. A moment of tense silence passed before Arthur repeated his question. "What kind of car is he driving?"

Arthur watched the wheels turning in Jake's mind. He was trying to figure out how to keep Arthur's name off the FBI's radar as anything more than the grief-stricken husband. Jake knew that trying to stop him was a fool's errand. He also had to know that Arthur getting involved was probably Sharon's best chance at coming out of this alive. "They think he's driving a gray Chevy Impala, late-seventies model, plates out of Socorro

County. Belongs to an eighteen-year-old kid who lives not far from where the van was found. Kid reported it missing late this morning. Thought his mom was going to be upset with him; that's why he waited so long. That waiting gave Kanesewah about a four-hour head start. News outlets will be reporting the vehicle description on the air soon, asking anyone who sees it to call their local law enforcement office."

"What makes the feds so sure he's heading south?"

"Because from Belen it's only three and a half hours to the Mexican border, so the law of averages favors that's where he's going. Kanesewah knows he jumped the gun with his last kill. Knows he fucked up. So if he's as smart as they seem to think he is, he'll run. Grabbing Sharon just gave him something to bargain with in case it doesn't look like he'll make it." Jake stood and picked his hat up off the table. He paused and gave his friend a sympathetic look. "I can't stop you from going after Sharon, because I'd be doing the same damn thing if it were me. But just do me a favor and be careful. If the feds can tie the other killings to this bastard, there are bound to be more bodies before this is over."

"Why do you say that?" Arthur asked, knowing full well the answer.

Jake put his hat on his head and cocked it a little to one side before resting his right palm on the butt of his holstered gun. "Because he enjoys it." He paused. "Guys like him just don't start killing like that for no reason. I bet he got his start a long time ago. Whatever set him off is what keeps him killing. And the fact that he's been able to keep it down to about one murder a year shows that he was able to keep his thirst in check." Jake opened the kitchen door and glanced back at Arthur. "If it is him, then he was able to quell his lust for a few years. Maybe there was something or someone that made him stop. Or maybe he was just lying low, biding his time. Maybe whoever had been filling whatever void he has couldn't fill it anymore. For whatever reason, he's going to kill again." Jake exhaled sadly. "And when he does … I just hope you've got Sharon back."

CHAPTER FIVE

Leonard Kanesewah took the last drag from his sixth cigarette in an hour before flicking it out the Chevy's window. He savored every curl of icy menthol as it swirled around inside his lungs while the radio brought the Four Corners area an up-to-the-minute report with the same information it had force-fed them ten minutes earlier.

The broadcaster's disembodied voice rehashed the story of the KZRV-TV news van being found in Polvadera, with cameraman Oscar Hirada dead inside from strangulation. The corner of Kanesewah's mouth twisted upward with the memory of how the Mexican had fought against the cable as it slowly cut that deepening furrow into his throat, crushing his larynx and sealing off his lungs from the outside world until he fought no more.

The broadcaster ended the story by repeating that KZRV's weekend news anchor and field reporter Sharon Keonie Nakai's whereabouts were still unknown. Kanesewah exhaled slowly and watched as the grayish smoke got sucked out his open window. Out of the corner of his eye, he caught his reflection in the rearview mirror. He watched as the twisted grin transformed itself into a satisfied smile.

The next movement of the media symphony featured the family of Renée Braun. Kanesewah imagined the girl's father standing before the throng of microphones and reporters, his wife sobbing at his side as he lectured the media on how the killer should be put down like the rabid animal he was. He also reassured them that he would make sure he was in the courtroom every day of the trial and standing front and center at the killer's execution. The broadcaster's voice returned, announcing that FBI Special Agent in Charge Frederick Thorne had stepped up to the microphone for a scheduled news conference that they were now joining in progress.

"At approximately nine o'clock this morning," Frederick Thorne began in a calm and measured manner, "the body of sixteen-year-old Renée Braun was found in a shallow grave in the Cibola National Forest by campers out for a morning hike. She had been brutally murdered. Forest rangers then contacted the county sheriff and the United States Bureau of Land Management. During their investigation, the Sheriff's Department discovered similarities to other murders committed over the past fifteen years and contacted the FBI."

The press room at the Gallup office of the FBI remained quiet as Thorne went on. "We believe the suspect, Leonard Kanesewah, to be heading south in a gray Chevrolet Impala to flee to Mexico with a hostage, Sharon Keonie Nakai." Thorne rattled off the license plate number as the microphones and cell phones recorded it quietly. "Mrs. Nakai, as you all know, is a well-respected reporter for KZRV-TV news, and her safety, while locating and apprehending Mr. Kanesewah, is our main concern. We have had no contact from Mr. Kanesewah and are already following up on several leads that have been called in to our mobile command post. We feel confident that this situation will be resolved quickly."

"What precautions are being taken in case he isn't heading south as you suspect?" barked a reporter.

"We are working very closely with all local law enforcement agencies in the Four Corners area, including the Navajo Nation Police, the New Mexico and Arizona State Police, and all pertinent sheriffs' departments." Thorne's answer then took on a more textbook tone—a ready-to-order statement filled with all the buzzwords that reporters and the oblivious public expected men in his position to recite in order to offer a false sense of order to a disordered world. "Now, I want to reassure the public that they are not in any danger, but should you see anything, please report it to authorities quickly and do not engage Mr. Kanesewah in any way. Now, if you'll excuse me …"

"Is it true that the girl was sexually assaulted?" one reporter called out.

Other reporters' voices sprang into action like a colony of gulls fighting over a bag of French fries. But apparently Thorne had left the room.

Kanesewah chuckled briefly, turned off the radio, and listened to the wind buffeting past the Chevy's open windows. Since the FBI had now given a description of the car, he would have to get rid of it sooner than he had planned. He checked the dash clock, hoping he still had enough time to make it to where she would already be waiting with her car. He was also glad that the noise from the trunk had finally stopped. All that kicking and muffled screaming had given him a headache. Now there was nothing but quiet and peaceful scenery approaching through the windshield.

He reached over to the passenger side of the front seat and grabbed the Nokia flip phone that he had found during a quick search of the glove compartment. He had made sure to keep it close at hand, resting next to his Marlboro hard pack. He had noticed how Special Agent in Charge Thorne had left out the part about the positioning of the girl's body, and the missing panties, and ignored the question about sexual assault. The feds were playing it close to the vest. He set the phone in his lap for a moment and pulled the pink panties with the little white bow from his pants pocket and sniffed them again. It had been quite a long time since he smelled that kind of sweet scent. He took another deep breath before shoving them back into his pocket with his thumb. He inserted the battery he'd removed from the phone the moment he found it in the glove compartment, knowing the FBI would be trying to ping the car owner's GPS, flipped it open on his lap, and pressed the center button to power it up. Then he quickly dialed her number.

"It's about time you called!" Gloria Sanchez said. "You're all over the fucking TV!" She paused. "Is it true what they're saying? That you killed that girl and all those others?"

"Baby, you know me," he said. "Do you think I could really do something like that? They're just trying to pin that shit on somebody, and they picked me because they've got nobody else. That's why we've gotta move. I need time to think of a way to fight their lies."

"I know a lawyer," Sanchez offered. "I could call him and—"

"That's great, baby," Kanesewah interrupted in a calm voice. "Just listen. I'll be there in a couple of hours or less, so be ready to move. You got all the stuff I told you to get?"

"Yeah, I got it all," Sanchez said. "Everything you told me—all packed and ready." Her voice brightened. "It's gonna be good, huh? You and me gettin' outta here and starting a life together—"

Kanesewah ended the call and cleared the number from the recent-calls list before resting his wrists on top of the steering wheel. He gripped the phone with both hands and twisted violently, snapping it in half. Seeing no traffic ahead or behind, he gave the bottom half of the phone a hard fling out the driver's side window. He watched as it flew across the highway and vanished into the desert scrub. He knew that the FBI would be trying to ping the car owner's phone, which was why he had turned it off the moment he found it in the glove compartment. That was also why he kept the call's length to a minimum. He let another mile pass before flinging the top half of the phone out the passenger-side window.

* * *

Arthur Nakai sat staring at the same empty beer bottle that had been sitting on his kitchen table since Jake Bilagody showed himself out over half an hour ago. On the screen of Arthur's mind, bits of memories were already playing themselves out like film shorts. He remembered first meeting Sharon as he walked through the massive D-shaped ruins of Pueblo Bonito in Chaco Canyon. He felt again the heat of that July day, contrasted with the cool in one of the lower rooms, where Sharon had stopped to study a mosaic of ancient fingerprints left by builders over nine hundred years earlier. She was startled when Arthur entered the room through the narrow passageway, then gave a bashful smile, realizing how silly she must have looked. Arthur politely smiled back, mesmerized by this vision in khaki shorts, whose raven-black hair fell in a long ponytail against the back of her white tank top. He followed her smooth, firm legs down to the brown leather Keen hiking boots with the dark coral laces and turned-down socks before winding his way back up to her face, unable to help noticing on the way how well she filled out every inch of the tank top. He knew instantly that she was Navajo, and his mind swirled as he tried to figure out whether she could be from the Towering House clan, the One-Walks-Around clan, the Bitter Water clan, or the Mud clan. Or maybe she was from one of the many adopted clans. If she happened to be from Towering House, his own clan, then this meeting was meant to be. He smiled apologetically and said he was sorry if he had frightened her.

The air that day had seemed charged with an awkward antic-ipation that Arthur had not felt in years. He feverishly groped about for something to dazzle her with. But, finding nothing that wouldn't make him seem a complete idiot, he began by speaking of the ruins and the fingerprints she had been looking at. From there, they wandered the ancient pathways of rooms, walked the narrow foot-wide ledge between two of the smaller kivas, and talked of their reasons for being there that day. As they walked toward the visitors' center parking lot, they discussed having dinner together at the Anasazi Inn in Farmington. Sharon was staying there for a couple of days while making a personal discovery trip to the canyon and several other Anasazi archeological sites.

Over steaks and a bottle of wine, he listened to her speak of the canyon and her reasons for exploring it. Her next jaunt, and the reason for her stay in Farmington, was to visit the ruins at Aztec. She had heard of the large reconstructed kiva there: how you could enter it and be transported back in time with the touch of a button that would fill the ceremonial chamber with the rhythmic sounds of beating drums and the haunting voices singing songs that would echo hypnotically around you as you stepped down to the dirt floor. How you could sit on the narrow ledge that circled the inner wall and feel its coolness as your mind and body drifted into thoughts of witnessing sacred tribal rituals.

As Arthur listened to her stories, his heart began to unlock with the softness of her voice, which became the key that released his soul. And the more she spoke, the more he fell into the mesmerizing depth of her eyes as she slowly began to weave her *álíít*, her magic, into his being. Then, at a moment known only to him, he began to fall in love.

That image soon dissolved into a starry autumn night as he sat stretched out across the rustic porch swing outside their bedroom window on the mesa, his boot heels resting on the far wooden arm of the swing, between the chains that held it suspended from the ceiling. The night was clear, and he could pick out the constellations easily. Sharon's wind chimes danced softly on the sage-filled breeze and sang a soothing tune as she lay in bed under their quilted comforter, watching satellite television. Arthur could neither hear the sound nor see the picture. He simply watched quietly as Sharon, with the comforter drawn up under her chin, gazed intently at the changing images on the screen. He watched how her hair transformed into different shades of black as the images flickered across the thirty-seven-inch flat panel. As soon as Sharon noticed him peering through the window, a small hand appeared from under the covers to wave playfully at him. He smiled back and waved just as Billy Yazzie's voice jerked him back into reality.

"Anything you need me to do before I leave, boss?"

Billy stood six feet tall and had one of those skinny mustaches it seemed every Navajo man tried to grow at some point just to see if he could. He was a muscular kid with a short black mop, and the youthful face behind the mustache had served him well with the *at'ééké* during his twenty-eight years on the rez. Girls always seemed to have a way of losing their wits around him. When he wasn't taking care of Arthur's horses, mending tack, and confirming reservations for vacationing guests, Billy spent his time filling the driver's seat of a big rig when there was work to be had. And that meant he worked for Arthur much more than he drove, because not a lot of driving work got doled out to young men like him. Seniority had always been the coin of the realm in the trucking industry, but for Native American drivers in the white-run firms, it was a catch-as-catch-can existence. You took what routes you were given and didn't complain—not if you wanted to keep driving.

"Sorry," Arthur said. "What did you say, Billy?"

"I said, is there anything you need me to do before I leave, boss?"

Arthur shook his head absently, not shifting his attention from the beer bottle. "No. That's all."

"You all right?" Billy's concern was genuine. It was all he knew how to be. "You need anything?"

"No." Arthur paused, then glanced up at the young man. "Go home."

Billy nodded and turned to leave.

"I won't need you for a while, Billy," Arthur added. "Something's come up."

Billy stopped at the kitchen door and turned. "I thought so," he said. "Captain B. wouldn't tell me why he was waiting for you. I asked him enough times. But that's cool. I've gotta run a load of steel up to Moab before pulling a Rocky Mountain double on to Coeur d'Alene. I was going to tell you when you got back today." He grinned. "I couldn't pass up two loads. Maybe one back, if I'm lucky. Man, I hate deadheadin'."

Arthur began to drift off again. Billy noticed. "You sure you're gonna be okay?"

Arthur looked up again from his slumped position in the chair. The beer bottle wasn't going anywhere. "You drive carefully, huh?"

Billy opened the kitchen door. "Sure, boss," he said, and closed it softly behind him.

The only noise now that gave life to the quiet house was the low hum of the refrigerator's motor while the tick-tock of the regulator clock measured time's never-ending spiral into tomorrow. Arthur watched a fly land on the lip of his dark-brown bottle. He watched it circle the rim before darting inside the neck of the bottle and then reappearing. It paused on the rim, almost as if studying him, and then buzzed away.

With a deep breath, Arthur forced himself up from the chair and wandered into the living room with no real thought to why. He sank into the sofa, picked up the remote that he had left on the adjacent seat cushion the night before, and thumbed it on. After the satellite was located and the usual prompt appeared, he pressed the SELECT button and found himself in the middle of an *Eyewitness News 4* report. He listened as the story unfolded about three brothers who were thought to be missing in the Carson National Forest since Friday. They had driven into Carson on a hunting trip, leaving nebulous plans with relatives. The morning rains had swelled into a storm that grew into a torrential downpour by Saturday night, and no one had heard from them in three days.

Three and a half million acres of forest, and a pickup truck lost somewhere in the middle of it. If the hunters had even a little bit of sense, they hadn't wandered too far from the pickup and would stay dry until someone found them. Surely, they had provisioned food and a few blankets. Then again, recalling some of the would-be hunters he had known in the past, he supposed not. The next image to appear on the LCD screen was a mug shot of Leonard Kanesewah over the left shoulder of anchorman Brett Parker.

Arthur stared at the photo as all sound fell away from the TV. To hell with this waiting, he told himself. If Sharon was going to be found, he was going to be the one to do it.

CHAPTER SIX

News anchor Brett Parker appeared visibly shaken. He paused briefly to regain his composure before continuing as Kanesewah's picture was replaced with a file picture of Oscar Hirada. "Police and the FBI also suspect Kanesewah in the kidnapping of our own Sharon Keonie Nakai, who was in Belen covering a story, and have now added aggravated kidnapping charges to Kanesewah's growing list of offenses." Sharon's head shot now replaced Oscar's. "Police located the *Eyewitness News Four* van around two o'clock this afternoon in the small town of Polvadera, about thirty-three miles south of Belen, with Oscar Hirada's lifeless body inside. FBI Special Agent in Charge Frederick Thorne has issued a statewide manhunt."

Gloria Sanchez sat on the stained and sagging couch, staring at the television from across the dingy room. Her legs were crossed beneath her, her left hand holding her right elbow as she chewed the tip of her right thumb. If they were lucky, they would soon be in Canada relaxing by a lake somewhere, drinking wine in a hot tub, because Leonard had to be innocent. He as much as said he was. This was just another way for the government to persecute Native people and keep them down as they always did.

Her thought vanished as she heard a car roll up the dirt driveway from the dirt street and come to a stop behind the small cinder-block house. Jumping to her feet, she punched off the television and stood in tense silence as the engine turned off. A car door opened and closed. Her eyes moved around the now darkened room, frantically searching for the duffel bag on the floor, by the pile of supplies Kanesewah had instructed her to collect. She ran to it and squatted down beside it. Zipping it open, she rummaged through it for the Smith and Wesson .38-caliber revolver she had stashed inside. Her fingers wrapped around it, and she crept to the rear of the three-room house. Flattening against the wall just left of the back door, she could feel her nostrils flare and contract with every nervous breath. Over her accelerating heartbeat, she heard the soft noises of internal tumblers as they rolled inside the twisting doorknob. Her eyes followed its counterclockwise rotation. Thumbing back the hammer of the .38, she could feel the moisture from her sweating palm on the knurled wooden grip. *Relax*, she told herself. *Breathe.* The door swung open to reveal a human shape moving in the doorway. When Leonard Kanesewah stepped into the small room, Gloria Sanchez thumbed the hammer down carefully.

Kanesewah spun at the click of the revolver's mechanism, and his big hand engulfed the weapon, jerking it from her grip as his other arm cocked to deliver a powerful blow.

"It's me, baby!" Sanchez shouted though her upraised hands. "It's me!"

Kanesewah's instinct for self-preservation seemed to relax as the voice and the face before him synchronized in his memory. Gloria Sanchez leaped into his arms and kissed him passionately, her hands gripping the back of his head and bringing his lips against hers. Kanesewah pushed the door to and locked it, then let his hands roam her body until she felt them grasp her firm buttocks and squeeze them roughly. Her breasts heaved against his chest with every hungry breath as their tongues met and Kanesewah lifted her from the floor and carried her to the bedroom.

* * *

Sharon awoke from her restless sleep the moment the car turned off the smooth pavement of Highway 191 onto what must have been a dirt road, judging by the bits of debris that rattled in the fender wells as the car moved slowly forward. There wasn't the washboard ripple she would have noticed on a graded dirt road, just the normal dips and bumps of an almost flat dirt surface. Knocking around in a dark trunk that reeked of oily rags and tire rubber, it was impossible to find a comfortable position on the ragged bit of filthy carpeting. She tried moving, but the stiff coax cable bit into her wrists and ankles, reawakening the pain that had abated earlier while she drifted off into fractured sleep.

Sharon remembered the man being in the van. And she remembered seeing Oscar's body sitting amid the recording equipment, his throat ringed with reddish bruising, the tiny petechial dots scattered across his eyes, the white cord of his earbuds still dangling from his ears, and the coax cable that had strangled him hanging loosely from his neck. He sat with his head angled to the left, arms loose at his sides, and legs outstretched before him in a V, as if he were only sleeping.

Sharon also recalled the man binding her wrists and ankles and throwing her into the trunk of a car where she heard the news report through the rear speakers. The name Leonard Kanesewah didn't ring any bells, but what did that matter now? She was here, and all that mattered was finding some way to extricate herself from this situation and get to safety.

She suddenly began to hyperventilate as fear and grief and rage churned inside her. *Control yourself,* she repeated over and over in her head. *You must maintain control.* Whatever was coming would come, so to keep herself alive, she must play the waiting game. And not knowing for how long this Kanesewah had stopped the car or where it had stopped, she would have to be ready to seize her chance to escape if that chance should present itself. Swallowing her thoughts, she conjured Arthur's face in her mind's eye. Had he been told by now? If so, it had to be Jake Bilagody who told him. And it would be all Jake could do to keep him from coming after her. And he *would* come after her.

CHAPTER SEVEN

Arthur Nakai killed the images coming from the flat-panel screen above the thick burl mantel of the river-rock fireplace. He tossed the remote onto the coffee table and watched it skid across the epoxied slab of redwood and off the opposite edge, where it bounced with a muffled thud on the woven rug. *Hell with it*, he thought.

Suddenly, the realization hit him that his wife had just become another two-minute story in the never-ending chain of two-minute stories that the Fourth Estate spoon-fed the viewing public each day. He sighed. Maybe Sharon should quit and leave it all behind. Perhaps it was too late for that? He shook off the feeling and looked around at the house that surrounded him. He felt incongruous in this place now filled with silence. And it wasn't the kind of relaxing silence that he welcomed at the end of a long day, but the inescapable, crushing kind he dreaded now that the world he took for granted had been so violently ripped apart. But now an awkward alone feeling began to settle in. Vanished were the smiles and laughter that had always given this sanctuary its life and its warmth. Gone the familiar things that meant she was here: the quiet breathing while she sat at the opposite end of the sofa reading; lying together under a blanket before a crackling fire and feeling her body close to his. It was as if a part of his soul had been ripped away, leaving nothing but emptiness and a newfound regret.

He stood up and began to walk around the empty house, giving no conscious thought to where his feet led him. He found himself in their bedroom on the second floor, staring into the bathroom where Sharon's toiletries sat just as she had left them. And her smell was there. He didn't know how, but the whispering hint of her perfume had managed to linger all these hours later, as if solely to torture him. He turned away and stared into their bedroom. The bed was made, as it always had been when left to her attention, the sheets smooth and precise and the pillows positioned as if some high-end designer had arranged them.

Leaving the bedroom, he walked down the short hallway, past the nursery door they had locked those few years ago. He paused briefly to let the moment pass, then stepped away from the door and moved back downstairs, through the living room, to the kitchen. He stared at their breakfast dishes languishing in the sink, rinsed but not yet washed. He opened the kitchen door, closed his eyes, and inhaled the cleansing aroma of sage, savoring its rejuvenating essence. Exhaling, he felt as though the harmony he spent years of his life achieving had now abandoned him. Without Sharon, he felt as lost as an asteroid tumbling aimlessly through the vastness of space.

Leaving the kitchen door open, he returned to the living room and lifted the chocolate suede leather pouch from its stand on the mantel. He cradled it carefully in his hands as he walked back into the kitchen, studying its almost two-foot length of ancient beadwork and bison fur, and the fringed leather end flap tied with two long, softened leather ribbons, each decorated with one blue and one turquoise bead and tied delicately at the ends. The flap's fringe sang with the gentle *ching* of small cone-shaped silver bells as he walked. Pushing open the screen door, he stepped out onto the long back porch and into the cooling late-afternoon air.

A pale moon floated high in the changing sky as if chasing the sun into twilight. As the swift tropospheric winds propelled a swath of Cirrus spissatus clouds across the sky in what seemed like time-lapse imaging, their shadows ran over the land on their march across the mesa. The screen door slammed shut behind him as he walked over and sat in the rocking chair that faced the swing on the opposite end of the porch. He tugged gently at the tan leather ribbons with the blue-and-turquoise beads and reverently turned back the flap with the jingling cones. He could smell the cedar even before his fingers reached inside the pouch and felt the hand-smoothed wood.

It had been a gift from his father when he was small. A gift passed down through four generations to his young hands. His great-great-grandfather had made it in the time before Custer was killed at Little Big Horn. Arthur marveled at the hand-carved masterpiece, from its sloping mouthpiece to its carved eagle's-head tip. He took a moment to adjust the carved block on the flute's nest and moistened his lips. A gentle breeze lightly tossed the thin leather bands that held the block in place as Arthur inhaled and placed the flute to his lips. The second he closed his eyes, the music took flight, and as his fingers answered its bidding. His heart and mind began to fill with the peace and harmony that would help guide him down the long road he now must travel.

As his song came to an end, Arthur opened his eyes and let the final note trail off into nothingness. Out of the corner of his eye, he noticed that Ak'is had managed to find his usual place on the porch and had been resting comfortably, listening to the tones cascading from his flute. Arthur smiled. He rested the flute across his lap and thought of Sharon's father in Kayenta. Had anyone told Edward? Jake had said nothing of that, so it was best to think no one had. If Edward had seen the news or been told by a neighbor, he would have called. Or was he simply too distraught to call? Arthur returned the flute to its pouch and stood. "You want to go see your grandfather?" he asked Ak'is.

The wolf-dog made no reply. Not even a perk of the ears or a lift of the eyebrows.

Arthur nodded. "I'll leave you some water, then." It would be better for him to make the 156-mile trip from White Mesa to Kayenta by himself. And he would have to do it tonight.

* * *

The two-and-a-half-hour drive from White Mesa to K-Town had given Arthur time to think about how to tell his father-in-law that his only daughter had been kidnapped by a lunatic.

The conclusion: there was no easy way. He would simply have to say it.

Since Arthur's father died, Edward Keonie had become more than a father-in-law. He would seek Edward out for his deep knowledge of Navajo tribal tradition and for his expertise with horses. And when an important answer eluded him, Edward was his mirror and his sounding board. Arthur rubbed his brow and rolled down the window of the Bronco to let the cold evening air help keep him awake. It was now after eight o'clock on what had been a very long day. He felt as though he had been chasing the sunset through the windshield of his truck and never catching up to it. He had watched it transform from a blazing fire to a seductive purple and mauve to black velvet canvas sprinkled with flickering diamonds that seemed to have been flung there solely to help him think.

He turned the rust-spotted Ford from Highway 160 onto 163 at the brightly lit Fina gas station and drove north to Canyon Drive, where he turned right and followed its winding path around a maze of manufactured homes to Juniper Street. This was the back way into Edward's mobile home community, and the easiest way get to his place. He turned left onto Juniper, which soon ran too quickly into Aspen, where he stopped to think some more. The truck idled. More thought. He was looking straight ahead at the grayish end of Edward's modular house, illuminated in his headlights, and he could feel his anxiety beginning to build. His mind drifted back to the day he and Sharon surprised her father with his birthday present, successfully prying him loose from his disheveled double-wide of forty years and replacing it with twenty-first-century living. Edward subscribed, body and soul, to the philosophy of minimalism. He didn't need all the trappings and distractions the rest of the world seemed to require. Arthur remembered moving his father-in-law's bed, small dresser, table and three chairs, two-butt sofa, and two arm chairs out to the small lawn before the old rig was hauled away and the new modular house was set in place and leveled on the concrete pad. For someone almost seventy years of age, he wouldn't have much to leave behind when he passed from this world to the next.

No lights were visible in either of the black faux-shuttered bedroom windows—just the wide beam of the Bronco's headlights. Edward's older Chevrolet pickup, dappled with spots of brown primer, sat off to the left in the dirt parking area just past the gate of the weathered plank fence. Arthur took a deep breath and drove straight across the street and parked by the tailgate of the Chevy. He switched off the engine and sat for a long moment before climbing out of the truck and closing the door. It closed with that hollow metal sound that trucks make when they reach a certain age. In that way, old trucks were a bit like people.

The night air seemed colder, crisper now, and the smell of the fry bread and wood smoke seemed trapped in the density of it. Arthur pulled the latch on the gate and swung it open. Once through, he closed the gate and walked up the dirt path, past the small satellite dish that hung on the face of the house, to the right of the main double windows. He took the two steps onto the small porch with one stride and knocked on the door.

Edward believed in a lot of the old ways, especially when discussing matters of great importance. For those conversations, he always used Diné. *"When I speak Diné I speak the truth,"* he had once told Arthur. *"When I speak in the tongue of the Bilagáana, I may become a pathway to speak lies."* This would be a night of speaking Diné.

Arthur glanced up at the moon and stars floating in the blackened sky and took another deep breath and let it out slowly. A few moments passed before the inside door swung open and his father-in-law stood before him. Under the head of white hair that seemed as fluffy as down was a creased face weathered by a lifetime of Four Corners sun. Edward's deep-set old eyes stared down a narrow nose flanked by prominent high cheekbones. The squash necklace that matched the bracelet on his right wrist captured the moonlight and seemed to take on a life of its own. Edward Keonie flicked on the porch light so his eyes could better focus on his son-in-law.

"Arthur." He smiled. "*Yá'át'ééh, shiye'.*"

Ever since Arthur and Sharon's *iigeh,* their marriage ceremony, Edward had always greeted his son-in-law as "my son." And Arthur had always greeted him as "my father."

"*Yá'át'ééh, shizhe'e,*" Arthur replied. "May I come in?"

"Of course," Edward said, opening the storm door that now seemed to have a few more holes in its screen than Arthur remembered. Edward closed both doors behind them and motioned toward the main room and the pair of worn recliners by the boxy television that threatened to crush the feeble particle-board nightstand. Arthur didn't say anything.

"Sit," Edward said. "It has been a boring night." They sat opposite each other. "My cable doesn't work. I've done all the nonsense they told me when I called them. 'Push this button, hold that button, now type this in. Are you using the right remote?'" He shook his head. "They'll have someone out here in two days between noon and four. Sometimes I wonder why I even bother with this thing. It's becoming more of a nuisance anymore and there's nothing really worth watching anyway—just that reality crap and a few decent dramas is all they have nowadays."

Edward took a rolled up pouch of tobacco from the hip pocket of his khaki jeans. Edward never offered any to Arthur, knowing he didn't smoke and couldn't stand the taste of chaw. Edward opened it, took out a hefty pinch and tucked it into his cheek, then rerolled the pouch and returned it to his hip pocket.

He spoke in Diné. "I sense that you are in great turmoil, my son. Is this right?"

Arthur nodded. "Sharon has been taken, my father." He studied Edward's face. Seeing nothing, he continued. "By a man named Leonard Kanesewah." Arthur told him the story. "The police believe he hasn't harmed her yet. They think he will most likely use her as a bargaining chip."

Edward sat with his eyes divulging no emotion. There was no hurt, no anger, and no impatience—nothing that would betray his thoughts. Arthur sat bewildered.

"I have seen this man you tell me of, in a vision," Edward finally said. "I did not know who he was or why he was shown to me. I saw only the blackness of his heart. Before, he traveled the path of life; now he travels the path of the dead. In my vision, I did not see my daughter."

"The police and FBI have roadblocks all over New Mexico

and Arizona," Arthur told him, "because they believe him to be heading to Mexico."

Edward shook his head and waved his right index finger. "As I have already told you, he now travels the path of the dead, yet he is not dead. The police are lost in the smoke of the demon, and it is blinding them." Edward waved his dark, leathery hand from side to side. "They will not find him. In my vision, I did not see my daughter."

Arthur waited.

Edward sat in the recliner with his forearms resting on the worn chair arms, his old hands hanging over the ends. He raised his right hand and tapped with the tip of his index finger next to his eye. "I have seen a brave warrior with a strong heart fighting this demon."

Arthur waited some more. The visions of an elder were said to be powerful and were to be heeded. "In my vision, the demon with the black heart is battled by a brave warrior with a strong heart. The battle is one of wits and cunning and is waged on a field of white, where the strong heart will overcome his enemy. The vision has shown me this." Edward paused, reached for a small coffee can on the table beside him, and spat into it. "You are the warrior with the strong heart, my son." Pause. "It is you who must fight this demon."

CHAPTER EIGHT

Sharon Keonie Nakai drifted into consciousness, helped along by the bouquet emanating from the stained sofa where she lay. She tried to move but couldn't. In place of the cable, a black nylon rope crossed over the top of one foot and under the arch of the other, then wound around her ankles and looped through the binding that held her wrists behind her back. Every time she moved her feet, it pulled her hands back, tightening the bonds. Her hands and feet tingled, and the duct tape covering her mouth smelled of adhesive and thick saliva, which had a nauseating effect every time her tongue tried to push between her lips.

The first thing tumbling through her foggy memory was that the car had come to a stop, a door had opened and shut, and then there was only the feeling of helplessness as she lay in the dark, smelling oily rags and tire rubber. She had no way of calculating how much time had passed or how far they had traveled before the trunk lid sprang open and the man stood above her, staring down and smiling. She remembered struggling with him as he pulled her from the trunk, and him dragging her toward the cinder-block house underneath the carport. And then she recalled the moment his big hand smacked the side of her head with a force that turned everything black.

She looked around the room. It was Navajo Housing Authority construction. Sand-colored walls, garage-sale mismatched chairs and sofa haphazardly arranged, windows covered in what appeared to be aluminum foil and duct tape. No telephone that she could see. She registered the location of the front door and how many foil-covered windows were visible. Then she looked for anything that could serve as a weapon if she somehow managed to get free of the ropes that bound her. She also noted the pile of camping gear, flanked by two duffel bags, in a corner of the room. Maybe one of them contained a gun, not that it would do her any good at the moment.

"What the hell did you bring *her* for?" an angry Latina voice said. "I mean, what the fuck?"

"She's our insurance policy," Kanesewah replied bluntly. "She stays."

Sharon's eyes moved to the woman's face as she leaned into view from the kitchen doorway and then disappeared.

"Your *insurance* is awake," the woman snapped.

Kanesewah stepped into the room, a stick of beef jerky moving in his mouth as he gnawed on the end. He stopped a few feet from the sofa, reached up and grabbed the moving jerky, tore a piece off, and chewed it. He squatted down in front of Sharon, both feet flat on the floor, and balanced his forearms on his knees, his head at a slight tilt as if he were examining her.

"You, me, and my woman are going to be leaving soon," he said, pointing at Sharon with the remaining bit of jerky. "And don't even think about running, because you can't. Those ropes are nice and snug. I've had a lot of practice." He popped the last piece of jerky into his mouth and chewed. "It's funny what turns a woman on these days. Tie 'em up and they get all hot and wet—that is, until they realize it's not foreplay. Then the ropes become more pain than pleasure because the more they struggle, the tighter they get. And when they finally lose strength from exhaustion, they strangle themselves. It's really something to watch. What I remember most is that they all died with their eyes wide open, staring at me while I watched them struggle for that last breath." He gave a dry laugh. "But you don't have to worry. I'm saving you for something special. You'll see." He reached out and gently caressed Sharon's cheek with the backs of his curled fingers. She didn't recoil—just tolerated his rough touch as it ran slowly down to her chin. He grabbed her jaw in his thick fingers, which smelled from the greasy jerky and set off her hunger. "And if you even try to signal anyone we come across for help, I will kill them. And then I will kill you, insurance or not. Do you understand?"

Sharon nodded.

"Good." His hand moved from her jaw to test the fullness of each breast as it filled his palm. Sharon watched as his breath quickened and his eyes locked with hers. "Like I said, I've got real sweet plans for you. And I don't want you to miss one minute of them."

CHAPTER NINE

Arthur Nakai's breath fogged in the cold morning air and mixed with the exhaust curling up from the rear of the Bronco as he loaded the back of the truck. Even after living here most of his life, he still hated these frosty mornings. And sometimes, as winter drew closer, the afternoons weren't much better with their icy winds and frigid temperatures. At times like this, when the skies were gray and the snow dappled the high desert like icing on a coffee cake, the damp air would creep into his body in search of a healed bone and make him remember the pain, while the cold penetrated deep enough to make his beating heart quiver in his chest. Although there was no snow on the ground, this was still one of those mornings, most likely enhanced by his lack of sleep. So he did as he always did on such mornings: simply turned up the collar of his shearling-lined denim jacket and tried to pay it no mind.

Movement on his left drew his attention as Ak'is stepped into the Bronco's headlight beams from the darkness beyond the corral. He moved quietly forward and stopped a short distance away. "Well," Arthur said, "I wondered where you'd run off to. Figured you had a hot date or something while I was gone."

Ak'is closed the distance, and Arthur felt the animal's solid, muscular mass against his legs. Then the wolf-dog wandered a few paces away and lay down on the cold, hard-packed ground. Resting his head on his front legs, he stared up at Arthur.

"You know something's wrong, don't you?" Arthur said. Ak'is raised his head and listened, adjusted his front paws slightly, stretched out one back leg behind him while keeping the other leg tucked warmly under his body. "Mama's not here and you're wondering why. Well, I have to go find her for us." Ak'is simply stared, twisted his head slightly to the left, and perked his ears. "Don't worry," Arthur promised. "I'm going to bring her back."

He finished loading the Bronco and tucked his .338 Winchester Magnum hunting rifle with its Nikon scope and leather scabbard beneath the faux Navajo blanket he used to cover the rear cargo area. The blanket was one of those mass-market forgeries produced in Mexico. He had picked it up out of pure necessity some years back, at a store in Santa Fe. The clerk had stared at him with a confused look but said nothing. It was the kind tourists always bought because most could never afford the traditionally woven real thing. When over 750 hours of weaving went into a blanket, there was a reason for the high cost of craftsmanship.

He picked up the carry-on suitcase Sharon had given him for when they traveled off the ground and slid it under the blanket with the rifle. His oilcloth duster went on top of the blanket before he slammed the tailgate and swung the spare tire carrier back into locking position. Pausing for a long look around, he smelled the sage and felt the cold crispness of the morning against his face. The cold air always had a way of reminding him he was alive. Looking up at the vast array of stars that filled the black vault above, he thought of First Woman, writing the laws with them until Coyote came along and, in his impatience, grabbed the blanket upon which she kept the stars and recklessly tossed them into the sky. Arthur hung his head in reflection. Perhaps one day he would become the teacher to a son.

He cleared his mind and climbed into the Bronco, closed the rear window, took the GPS from his coat pocket, and tucked it into the glove box along with his night-vision binoculars. The two Glock 19C pistols—one holstered on his right hip, the other nestled in a shoulder sling under his left arm, brought with them the comfortable familiarity of his past. Ak'is now stood steadfast in the headlight beams, eyes shimmering like two golden rings. Arthur fastened his seat belt and waited for him to move. When he didn't, Arthur shook his head and opened his door. Ak'is trotted up and jumped in, lunged across his lap, and sat in the passenger seat. Arthur just looked at him, closed the door, and began the drive to Shiprock. At least he would have someone to talk to.

As he picked his way through the darkness that covered the mesa, he had a thought and abruptly changed course, toward the small hogan of Harold Tsosie. He stopped and honked twice. That had always been their signal for Harold to come out.

Harold was an elder who lived in the old way. Long ago, when he was a young man, he had built this cone-shaped hogan of angled branches covered in bark, grass, and earth that rose to a single smoke hole at the highest point. This was said to please the sun god, Johano-ai, as it shone on the dwelling, because it would look down upon it and see a reflection of itself. The single wood door faced east to receive the sun's blessings each morning and catch its warming rays.

Harold Tsosie had always loved horses. He had trained them many years ago, when he worked as a young man for a ranch that had long since faded into memory. Now he could remember those days only with a fondness that came from old age. Harold didn't think much of motorized vehicles, either. He never trusted anything that would cost you more money to keep running than you could get if you sold it. His only transportation was and had always been a horse he kept in a small corral and shelter near his hogan. There had been many horses, but always only one Harold.

Arthur spent a few minutes working out the arrangements with Harold to check on his horses while he was away, explaining that Billy Yazzie would be hauling a load and unable to tend to them. Harold told him not to worry, that it would be an honor to care for them.

The old Ford turned south onto Highway 170 just as Arthur cracked a window to let out the built-up heat that was starting to bake him. Ak'is kept a watchful eye out the windshield, panting lightly.

Arthur's mind began to work through what Edward had spoken about the night before. During the drive back from Kayenta, he had been too tired to push his mind to make sense of it. As he passed Four Corners Regional Airport in the predawn, the lights of the airfield glowed softly behind the small scrub-brush hills on his left. His mind continued to run through multiple scenarios as he approached the traffic lights where La Plata Highway met Highway 64. Turning west onto 64, he got the Bronco up to speed on the small incline that angled away from the airport as the fenced-in lot of Singleton's Mobile Homes slid by on his right. Arthur smiled, remembering the day he and Sharon had gone there to purchase Edward's manufactured house.

Arthur understood that the feds were counting on Kanesewah to head south, but Edward's vision had spoken of one who *traveled the path of the dead, yet he is not dead.* North was all that could mean, Arthur figured, since one traveled the distance of life as the sun travels the sky, from east to west. But when making the transition after death, one ascended from south to north. It was something, but it still gave him really nowhere to start and no real lead to where on earth Kanesewah would be heading. All he could do now was hope that Jake Bilagody had new information that would be worth something to him when he got to Shiprock. Something a little more solid than an old man's dream.

CHAPTER TEN

The flags strung from the four poles outside the Shiprock District Navajo Nation Police station waved in the wind as Jake Bilagody parked his beefy new Suburban in the long parking lot opposite the Wells Fargo Bank across Highway 491. He lurched slowly out of the truck feeling more tired than usual and flexed his hands against the arthritic stiffness that always seemed to hit him in the morning. But this morning, even his badge seemed to weigh him down. Or maybe it was the fact that he had managed to get only four hours' sleep in his own bed after his drive back from Window Rock last night. In by 1:00 a.m. and up by 5:00 a.m. was no way to live at his age.

Ever since the Window Rock chief of police resigned, citing political differences with the tribe, Jake and the other captains from the six districts had been pulling double duty as acting chief for the entire Navajo Nation while running their own district offices. He wondered when the decision would be made to promote someone into the position full time or else locate a candidate outside the force, who would be happy to accept the over sixty-three thousand dollars a year they were offering as salary. Presently, all he was hoping for was to put a stop to the commuting.

After getting himself a hot mug of black coffee from the break room, the commuting police chief sat behind his desk and began going over some of the community's complaints about the poor response times to reported crime. He flexed his fingers again, remembering how, when he spoke before the Navajo Nation Council's Law and Order Committee, he had stressed that the department was currently facing several challenges. He had explained that whereas most rural areas of the United States had about four officers for every thousand people, his officers were stretched terribly thin due to the vast area they had to cover. In the Navajo Nation, they had about half an officer for every thousand people. And you could not police effectively with that kind of ratio, he had explained to deaf ears. He laid down the papers and wrapped his stiff fingers around the coffee mug, letting its warmth sink through to his bones. He had just taken a mouthful of coffee when Special Agent in Charge Frederick Thorne of the FBI sauntered through his open office door.

"Any luck so far?" Jake asked.

Thorne carried off the square-jawed, Dick Tracy look well for a young man—so much so that Jake wondered why he hadn't become a Calvin Klein model. The pay was surely better. Thorne held one hand against the long black tie that matched his crisp black suit and sat in one of the wooden chairs that faced the chief's desk. "Not yet," he replied. "But I have every confidence my agents will locate Mr. Kanesewah and take him into custody, dead or alive."

Bilagody swallowed another mouthful of coffee. "Aren't you forgetting he has a hostage?"

"Not at all," Thorne replied. "Mrs. Nakai's safety is of the utmost importance. I only meant that if Kanesewah wants to make the hard choice, we are prepared to accommodate him."

"Of that I have no doubt," Jake said. "But this isn't the Old West anymore. We don't generally shoot the suspect as our first option."

Agent Thorne smoothed a pant leg with his hand and disregarded the comment. "I hope Mr. Nakai isn't going to be a problem. I don't want him getting involved in a federal investigation and making things worse. You have spoken with him as I asked?"

Jake rocked back in his office chair and interlocked his fingers across his belly. "He's still in shock," he said flatly. "But he knows how things work, and promises me he'll stay out of it and let you do your job."

"For his sake, I hope so," Thorne replied. "And for yours."

Jake rocked his chair forward. "Don't threaten me, Agent Thorne. I'm old enough to be your father, and I've been in this district too long to put up with that. And let me remind you that you're on Navajo land at our invitation, no matter what crimes the FBI thinks it's responsible for."

Agent Thorne stiffened. "I don't deal in threats, Chief. I deal in facts. And if Arthur Nakai even looks like he's getting involved in this, I will haul his ass in so fast, he'll be too dizzy to figure out where he is."

Jake folded his arms on his desktop. "If Arthur Nakai gets involved, Agent Thorne, it'll be you who can't figure out where he is."

Thorne's eyes rolled. "Look, I know all about his background. I've read his military and Homeland files. And I understand why he may feel the need to interfere, but you need to control him."

"*Control* him?" Jake said. "If it were my wife some lunatic had kidnapped, a whole damn Bureau full of suits wouldn't be able to stop me from trying to get her back." Jake lowered his head and ran his tongue between his teeth and lower lip as he looked up at Thorne. "Just because I know the man personally doesn't mean I can control him any more than I can control the wind. I can promise you that."

* * *

Thorne's reply was interrupted as Arthur Nakai appeared in the doorway of Jake's office, carrying a large insulated cup of coffee. He had stopped for gas at the Fina station on the way into Shiprock. He liked their strong coffee, but it needed a lot of cream to tame it.

"Promise him what?" Arthur said.

"Arthur," Jake said. "We were just discussing you. This is Special Agent Frederick Thorne up from the Gallup FBI field office. Special Agent Thorne, Arthur Nakai."

Thorne stood briefly and the two politely shook hands.

"I figured the FBI was here when I saw that menacing black Suburban parked outside," Arthur said. "You know, you guys should really go for something a little less conspicuous. Maybe a matte-black finish instead of the glossy paint job—get that whole *Agents of SHIELD* thing going for you."

Frederick Thorne grinned wryly but did not respond to the barb. Arthur walked past him and sat on the low credenza filing cabinet by the window, sipping his coffee. Maybe he had used too much cream.

Arthur sliced into the uneasy silence with a question to the FBI. "What are you doing to find my wife?"

Thorne stuck out his chin to loosen the collar of his starched white shirt. "We are doing everything we can to facilitate the apprehension of Leonard Kanesewah and bring about the safe return of your wife."

"Couldn't have put it more bureaucratically myself," Arthur replied. "You figure on finding her in this office? Because if you do, I don't think you're really doing *everything* you can."

Thorne placed his hands on the chair arms and stood up, squaring off to face Arthur. "Look," he began, "I understand how you feel—"

Arthur rose from the credenza, coffee in hand, and again disregarded the Navajo taboo against interrupting someone speaking. This was getting to be a habit. "I hardly think you do, Agent Thorne," he said, "so don't presume to tell me you know how I feel."

"I think Agent Thorne can rephrase that a little better, Arthur," Jake offered, trying his best to diffuse the situation. He flexed both hands. They were starting to feel cold and stiff again. "Isn't that right, Agent?"

Thorne gave a sideways look to the chief. "What I meant was, I can imagine how you must feel." He slid his hands into the pockets of his dark slacks, if for no other reason than to have something to do with them. "We have been following up on every lead coming in ever since this hit the news sources, and I've got men stretched from here to the Mexican border trying to locate him."

"And my wife," Arthur added.

Thorne exhaled, nodded. "Of course. Her safety is of the utmost importance."

"So you've said." Arthur sipped his coffee and swallowed. Maybe he would add some sugar next time. "But more than forty-eight hours have already passed. And once Kanesewah hit the hardball, any chance you had of locating him fell to some average citizen spotting him eating a cheeseburger or taking a leak." Arthur paused. "And your chances are getting more remote by the minute."

"Hardball?"

"Asphalt, blacktop, paved road," Arthur rattled off. "Once they hit that, your chance of tracking them went to hell."

Thorne seemed to study his shoes for a moment, then looked up at Arthur. "Then I guess it's good the FBI has something called modern technology among its many assets."

Arthur smirked and kept quiet about Edward's vision. He knew the FBI wouldn't put any faith in anything they couldn't slap a label on and shove into an evidence box. "I knew cocky bastards like you when I was in the sandbox," Arthur said, glancing at Jake before returning his attention to Thorne. "They never lasted more than a few weeks."

"Don't underestimate me, Mr. Nakai." Thorne's face turned deadly serious. "I've seen my fair share of action—maybe not in-country like you, but I've seen it just the same."

Arthur said, "Let me break it down Barney-style for you. I

don't know whatever criminal justice class they pulled you from, but what you've seen and what I've seen are not the same. I've had AK rounds rip through corrugated metal and fly past my head like a swarm of bees. I've seen an eight-year-old boy pick up an RPG and had to take him out before his finger could pull the trigger. I've carried my brothers back after having their legs blown off by IEDs. So, you see, I'm not especially interested in what you've seen."

Thorne took a deep breath, then turned to Jake. "Be sure to keep me informed if anything should come your way, Chief."

Jake stood and offered a hand across his desk. They shook. "The minute I hear anything," he said.

Thorne started to offer his hand to Arthur, who pretended not to notice as he turned to look at nothing outside Jake's office window. Thorne buttoned the second button of his suit jacket and walked out.

A few seconds passed before Jake said, "Well, that sure was like watching two kids pissing to see whose stream could reach the electric fence."

"Don't you start," Arthur replied.

Jake chuckled.

"Did he give you have anything new?" Arthur asked.

"Just what he told you." He nodded toward Arthur's coffee cup. "You want a refill on that?"

Arthur downed the last dregs. "Is it fresh? I don't drink tar, and I know how cop coffee can taste."

Both men filled their cups in the break room, Arthur adding three sugars and an inch of cream while Jake seemed satisfied with black. Arthur motioned with his head toward the parking lot, and they stepped outside into the brisk morning air.

Shiprock had begun stirring with signs of life, and Arthur watched as Ak'is stood guard in the front passenger seat, occasionally getting a whiff of something interesting filtering through the windows Arthur had left slightly open beneath the vent visors.

"You'd tell me if you had anything to go on, right, Jake?" Arthur said, sipping his cop coffee.

"You know I would," Jake replied. "But my question to you is, do *you* have any information for *me*?"

Arthur looked south toward the empty parking lot of the Begaye Flea Market. The vendors were gearing up for the swarm of locals and tourists that would be coming throughout the day, searching for unheard-of bargains from would-be relic sellers willing to part with a priceless artifact at a discounted price. "I went to see Sharon's father yesterday. He told me he'd had a vision."

"What did his vision reveal?"

"Just crazy Navajo talk," Arthur said, dismissing it with a shake of his head. If it led him anywhere, he would need time to figure it out himself. "Nothing you would call a mind-blowing lead or anything."

"Your father-in-law is an elder," Jake said. "I was always taught to listen to my elders and respect their knowledge for there was always a great significance in what they had to say. What did Edward tell you?"

"He told me that Thorne and all his men stretched from here to the Mexican border are being blinded by the smoke of the demon."

"Uh-huh." Jake finally sipped his coffee. "That all?"

"That's it. I told you it was just crazy talk. What's up with your hands?"

Jake removed one from his coffee mug and flexed it. "Arthritis, probably. I'm thinking of buying one of those creams you see advertised on TV. Who do think I should trust, Johnny Bench or Chuck Woolery?"

Arthur stared. "Who?"

Jake just shook his head. "Never mind." He noticed the slight bulge in Arthur's denim jacket, and the tip of the tactical holster peeking out from under the hem. "You packing your Glocks?"

Arthur glanced down. "You noticed, huh?"

"It's kind of my thing," Jake said. "Trained eye, and all." He glanced through the rear window of the Bronco, noticed the scope of Arthur's rifle visible from under the blanket. "Goin' hunting, are you?"

"Thought about it. I figured maybe hunting elk in Colorado would keep me occupied and out of the FBI's way."

Jake smiled knowingly. "First season in Colorado for hunting elk with a rifle doesn't start till October twelfth this year. This is only the first. You must mean moose."

"Yeah, what I said. Moose."

"Thought so," Jake said.

CHAPTER ELEVEN

Gloria Sanchez switched off the Buick's headlights as the early morning sun spilled over the snow-capped peaks of the Wind River Range, washed down across the fertile valley floor, and pushed its way up the eastern side of the Wyoming Range. Leonard Kanesewah had fallen asleep in the passenger seat a short time after leaving Cruel Jack's Truck Stop in Rock Springs. He had correctly predicted it to be sparsely populated thanks to the expansive Flying J Center beyond it. They had stopped just long enough to fill the Regal's tank with gasoline and move on, keeping their visual exposure to a minimum.

They had abandoned the small cinder-block house just after midnight, heading north on 191. Now, after hours of tiresome driving to the monotonous drone of the Buick's fresh tires, the only sound keeping Gloria Sanchez awake was Leonard Kanesewah's thunderous snoring.

As they drove out of Pinedale, past the monolithic stone pillars and massive log timbers of the Hampton Inn, Sanchez reached up to adjust the rearview mirror and check on their unwilling passenger. Her vision was partially obstructed by the back of the front seat, so she twisted her head around over her right shoulder. Sharon was lying still and quiet under the blanket on the back seat. *Of course the bitch could sleep*, she thought. Why not? And why was she even here in the first place? Behind them, she caught a glimpse of Gannett Peak's nearly fourteen thousand feet, filling the rear window. She remembered hearing stories of the glaciers that crawled through its rocky valleys, and of the private plane from Minnesota that had crashed somewhere up there one year in late October. The searchers had picked up the ping from the plane's transponder, but it seemed lost among all the canyons, gullies, and boulder fields at that elevation. When the plane was finally located in early November, the father and his three sons had perished.

Gloria Sanchez pushed the rearview mirror back to where it belonged as her thoughts centered on the nagging bladder she had been ignoring for the past three quarters of an hour. She would have stopped at the Phillips 66 in Pinedale if she hadn't feared Kanesewah's wrath for taking a chance on being recognized by anyone who had read a newspaper or watched a TV in the past couple of days. She reached over and poked him in the left arm. "Hey. Wake up!"

When he didn't stir from his slumber, she poked him harder.

"Hey!" she said. "Wake the fuck up!"

"What the fuck, woman!" he growled. "Stop poking my ass."

"I've gotta pee."

"Well, sucks to be you."

"We're gonna have to stop," she said. "I've been holding it for almost an hour."

Kanesewah's face grimaced as he sat up in the passenger seat, rubbed his face with both hands, and then looked around. "Where the fuck are we?"

"Wyoming," Sanchez informed him. "We just left Pinedale. We're making good time."

Kanesewah stretched, inhaled deeply, and let out a long, leisurely groan. "Wait till we get a little farther out of town first and find a place off the highway. There's gotta be a turnoff somewhere."

Gloria Sanchez agreed and hoped her bladder would understand.

They passed a scattering of houses out by Route 352 and continued past the point where 191 merged with 189 and continued north. The dry grass of the gently rolling landscape had turned a dormant brown, and the morning sun that now filled the robin's-egg sky made her pull the visor down. The road dipped and then curved around the knob of a small hill, revealing a large green-roofed log home and barn that were overshadowed by a bigger hill behind the first. Leonard Kanesewah studied the terrain intently as Sanchez maneuvered the car. Neither spoke. After they crossed Forty Rod Creek, a dirt road appeared off to the right.

"Pull off up here on the right," he said, breaking the silence. "See where that goes."

Sanchez slowed and made the turn. They bumped over the cattle guard, then down the winding dirt road that led eastward before crossing the creek again and heading into the open range beyond Forty Rod Reservoir. Sanchez continued to follow the tire-worn double track, its every bump and dip reminding her of her bladder's plight. A few more miles went by before the road became little more than a wagon trail that angled abruptly north by a thick stand of cottonwoods.

"Follow the tree line," Kanesewah said. "There'll be water close by."

"I just hope there's a place for a girl to take a piss," Sanchez replied, following the cottonwoods.

The line of trees came to an end near another creek that cut across the open land like a vein of icy clarity. Kanesewah said, "Find a place to pull into the trees. Feds could have a bird in the air."

Sanchez maneuvered the car among the trees, turned off the ignition, and looked around. "Where the fuck you suppose I'm gonna take a leak?"

"I don't give much of a shit where you go," Kanesewah said. "You're the one who's gotta piss. Go squat behind a tree or something. It isn't like someone's gonna see your bare ass out here."

Gloria Sanchez grabbed the door handle angrily and got out with a parting "Fuck you."

* * *

Leonard Kanesewah felt the car shake as the door slammed. He watched as she walked in front of the car with her middle finger extended and headed deeper into the stand of trees. He pushed in the dash lighter, took the pack of cigarettes from his shirt pocket, and tapped one out. He had a good two-day lead on the

Federal Bureau of Incompetence. While the feds were spending all their time pissing in the New Mexican wind, he would be pushing well into Montana. All they had to do now was keep moving by night and lie low during the day, like those smugglers running drugs or illegals out of Mexico.

The lighter popped, and he pressed the glowing rings against the tip of his cigarette and took a long drag. If they could make it through Montana, then all they had to do was get across the Canadian border.

* * *

When the cigarette smoke reached Sharon Nakai, she held her breath as long as she could, hoping her captor would roll down a window. He didn't, and when at last she had to breathe again, her lungs rebelled. The duct tape over her mouth redirected the spate of coughing through her nose, stinging her sinuses with smoke and saliva.

Kanesewah laughed as he turned in the front seat, smoldering cigarette dangling from the left corner of his mouth. "Smoke bothering you?"

Sharon nodded, eyes watering.

"Thought so," he said, and turned back in his seat just as his woman crossed in front of the car again.

She yanked open the door, climbed in, and slammed it even louder than before. "Thanks a lot," she snapped. "I could have got snakebit or something out there!"

"Well," he said, grinning, "if you had gotten bit on that

sweet ass of yours, you *know* I would have enjoyed sucking out the poison."

The woman's anger transformed instantly into a sickeningly adolescent giggle. Leaning over, she removed Kanesewah's cigarette from his lips and kissed his mouth. Sharon listened as the kiss devolved into a chorus of moans that ended in the woman replacing the cigarette in his mouth.

The two stared at each other, and the woman licked her lips and, with a playful grin, leaned forward. Sharon heard the unmistakable sound of a zipper and watched the woman's head disappear below the seat back. The thought of what she was about to hear made her both revolted and uncomfortable. She saw Kanesewah's head relax against the bench seat's headrest and saw the slowly twisting tendril of smoke hit the tan roof liner and roll outward like a miniature mushroom cloud. The front passenger window went blessedly down, and he rested his right arm on the door and began breathing in short, shuddering gasps. Amid impassioned sighs and moans from both of them, the woman sped up the movements that would bring about a groaning, writhing end to this voyeuristic nightmare.

When the woman's head rose above the seat back, she turned and smiled at Sharon. Then, adjusting the driver's sun visor, she opened the vanity mirror, patted her lips with a tissue, and applied a fresh coat of red lipstick.

Kanesewah contentedly tucked himself away and yanked up his zipper. "Where's the map?" he said.

"In the glove box, like you told me," she replied.

Sharon heard the latch pop and the glove box door fall open, then some rummaging through loose papers. The glove box door slammed shut.

"Why don't you see if our insurance needs to piss. You two can do some female bonding while she's squatting."

The woman slapped the sun visor back into place and gave him an annoyed look. "Let's go, honey," she snapped, and got out. Jerking open the door behind the driver's seat, she studied Kanesewah's handiwork for a moment. "I'll have to untie your fucking straitjacket," she said. "She can't just bunny-hop over to a tree, you know."

Kanesewah stopped flipping through the narrow pages of the American Highway Digest Atlas and said over his left shoulder, "Then, just flip her over and fucking untie it."

Sharon squirmed to turn around on the back seat so the woman could untie her ankles. As she struggled to sit up, her feet and ankles rejoiced at the freedom of unrestricted blood flow. Sharon raised her hands, but the woman just grabbed her left arm and yanked her out of the car.

"Okay, chica, here's the deal," the woman said, leading her through the stand of cottonwoods. "I'm gonna drop your pants and undies so you can take a piss. I'll keep you right side up, but I'm not putting my hand between your legs. You piss on your pants, it's gonna suck to be you."

"You're not going to untie my hands?"

"Fuck no!" she snapped, and pulled Sharon's slacks and panties to her ankles. "Now, get to it."

Sharon nodded and squatted down, with the woman's hands on her shoulders for balance. Without appearing interested, she tried to take in as much information from their surroundings as she could. The mountains rising to the northwest must be the Absaroka Range—too far west for the Bighorns. For the past few hours, she had been taking quick glances out the back-seat window, looking for a road sign, the orientation of a distant mountain range, a name on a small-town storefront—*something* to give her some notion of where she was. But the angle of her head had made identifying anything all but impossible. All she knew for certain was that based on the morning sun, they were heading north, in a different car from the one Kanesewah had driven to the small house. They were still in Wyoming, but soon enough they would be in Montana. And on its far side, Glacier Park and the border—and, one way or another, the end of her journey. But Arthur would find her first. He had to.

CHAPTER TWELVE

Arthur sat at the intersection of Highways 491 and 64, staring through the windshield into the now bustling Begaye Flea Market parking lot. While the traffic light glared a harsh red, he looked over the patchwork of advertising banners that decorated the chain-link fence separating the parking lot from the intersection. One seemed to speak his language. The Nataani Nez Restaurant was offering a lunch buffet and drink for eight dollars. If it were any other day, he would take them up on it, but not today.

Off to his right, standing like a proud sail in the vacant corner lot, a large wooden sign announced the upcoming Northern Navajo Nation Fair, scheduled to begin in a few days. It was the oldest of the nation's fairs, and the most traditional. Sharon had always made a point of attending each year and bringing home something handmade to grace a wall or shelf. Smiling at the memory as the light changed to green, Arthur swung the Bronco into an arcing left turn that took it onto 64, toward Farmington.

Behind him, he heard a diesel engine straining against its heavy load. He was noticing how the truck's cab rocked in the mirror when his cell phone broke into its annoying factory ringtone. He had always meant to change it but hadn't been able to pick a tone he could tolerate from the lame list that the manufacturer provided. And the thought of paying actual money for a few seconds of ringtone seemed ridiculous. He pulled the phone from his jacket pocket and tapped ACCEPT with his thumb. "*Yá'át'ééh*, Billy!" he answered.

"Hey, boss," Billy began excitedly, "I was on my way up to Moab, you know, like I told you, and I saw the car!"

"What car?"

"From the news this morning. At least, I think it might be. I couldn't actually see the license plate, but it's the right make and color."

Arthur's thoughts of ringtones vanished. He checked all three mirrors to make sure none of Shiprock's finest were lurking nearby. Then he angled the Bronco over the sand-filled curb, across the empty sidewalk, and down onto the gravel road in front of the small red-and-white trailer that was the Injury Law Center. Throwing the truck into park, he said, "Where are you?"

"Across the border in Utah," Billy said. "About five miles north of the Mexican Water Chapter House, there's a handful of older NHA houses on the east side of 191. I just happened to glance over to check out this girl washing a car, and that's when I saw it. It's behind the third house. The back end is all you can see, but like I said, boss, it's the right make and color." Billy's signal faded briefly. "You want me to go back and check it out?"

"No, don't," Arthur said. "Too dangerous. And you could be

wrong. I know where you're talking about, but it'll take me about an hour to get there. You just keep driving and make your run. I'll check it out."

"Gotcha, boss." Billy paused. "I'm worried about Mrs. Nakai. I hope they find her before anything …" He let his words trail off.

"Did you call the police?" Arthur asked.

"No way, boss. First person I called was you."

* * *

The drive took a little longer than the hour Arthur had calculated. Driving up 191, he passed several tired-looking oil pumpjacks, rocking like big green drinking birds in the Ute land that flanked the highway. Much less of an eyesore were the three hundred photovoltaic pumps that the Utes had put in to replace the windmills pulling water from the ground. Beyond the faithfully bobbing pumpjacks, he came across a Navajo man, an elder, in a tattered wool coat with the collar turned up against the wind, walking a string of six cattle along the roadside. The cattle maintained a straight line, as if plodding to whatever tune the old man was singing, and neither they nor the old man paid him any attention as his truck roared by.

After leaving behind the Mexican Water Chapter House turnoff four and a half miles earlier, Arthur could pick out the small cluster of Navajo Housing Authority houses Billy Yazzie had mentioned. Ak'is had his snout thrust out the cracked passenger-side window, his olfactory sense surely overloaded by the exciting array of new smells. Arthur slowed as he approached the beige houses of uniform design, and studied them as he drove by. Sure enough, half hidden behind the third house was the gray eighties Chevy, just as Billy had described. He continued down the road another mile or so before turning around and heading back.

It was a small group of cinder-block structures, five on each side of the hard-packed dirt street, all of them painted to match the sere beige landscape and reflect the heat of the desert summer. Arthur drove up the dirt entrance, turned right, and parked by the farthest house, where smoke belched from the stack of a woodstove. He turned off the engine and told Ak'is to stay, then got out.

Looking at the vastness of the desolation surrounding him, he had to wonder how this spot came to be chosen over infinite others he had driven past since crossing the Arizona-Utah line. He noticed the large, still-muddy area where the car-washing girl had caught Billy's eye. Scanning the small tract of homes, he figured either no one had noticed his presence or no one cared, because no one had made themselves known as he walked up the dirt street toward the third house. Stepping closer, he noticed that all the house's windows were covered with aluminum foil. That recalled two possibilities from his Border Patrol days: either the residents were protecting their brains against alien or governmentally aimed microwaves, or it was a house used for making and/or stashing drugs. And he knew which one was more likely.

After flattening himself against the southern wall of the third house, he drew the compensated Glock 19C from his shoulder holster and thumbed the safety off. Pulling back the hammer, he crouched to pass beneath one of the foil-shrouded windows. After approaching the corner cautiously, he peered around it and saw the gray Chevy with Socorro County plates. The twin streaks of a jet pushed across the sky, disappearing as it passed above the wall of heavy rain he had seen marching in from the west. The wind managed to stir up some dust that swirled past him, chased by the faint rumblings of distant thunder rolling across the open land. But there was still no sound from the house. No radio, no TV, no voices. Just silence. He turned the corner, stepped up to the car, and placed the palm of his left hand on the hood. Cold. Inside it, he saw nothing interesting. Just a bundle of keys left in the ignition, and an open ashtray full of cigarette butts. Both front windows had been left down.

Arthur stepped to the back door of the small house and wrapped his hand around the tarnished brass knob. It turned freely. He heard the latch mechanism shift and cautiously opened the door. The first thing that hit him was the rank smell of stale food and the buzzing of flies. He moved cautiously through the house. In the kitchen, he found a pile of enough unwashed dishes in the cheap stainless-steel sink for what looked like three people, and a dozen roaches scurried that about when he disturbed them. The bathroom wastebasket held a used tampon, along with the wrapper from a new one. Sharon had stopped using those years ago as a result of a story concerning toxic shock she had done, so he knew who it didn't belong to. A small crumb of beef jerky lay on the floor by a dilapidated couch in the living room. He slipped the Glock back under his left arm. The house was empty.

The tampon meant Kanesewah now had another woman

with him. *Where did she come from? How did she fit into all this?* Outside again, Arthur started his methodical search by carefully stepping around the stolen car. He cut three signs that assured him of Sharon's continued existence. The first was a male footprint, probably a size twelve or thirteen, that made a tire tread pattern with a crescent cut in the heel. That would be Kanesewah. The second was a smaller footprint that could be a size seven or eight. This track was clearly a pair of cowboy boots, with three sweeping lines that ran across the Justin Gypsy logo on the ball of the foot and had a protruding crescent line, evident from the indentation in the dirt that ran from the outside forward edge of the heel toward its curving rear edge. That would be Kanesewah's woman, because the third track was unmistakable. It was the small D-shaped heel and large teardrop ball, both showing the minuscule horizontal lines of Sharon's Michael Kors Elisa pumps. He had been with her when she bought them. He squatted to get a better look at its depth and pattern. The prints weren't what he would expect to see if she were walking—more as if she was hopping and then being dragged after a brief pause. He was sure she had been bound at the ankles so she wouldn't run, which would mean her wrists were probably bound as well. But the set of tracks leaving the house meant she was alive and had been put into another car—probably one that Kanesewah's woman drove.

The other car had been facing the opposite direction from the Chevy, judging from the dirt kicked up in its wake as it sped away. From the aggressive directional tread pattern and the siped tread blocks, the car likely had fresh Firestone Winterforce tires. Funny the things one remembered from tracking on the border. He could tell a Goodyear from a Goodrich, though not a burgundy from a maroon, as Sharon was always quick to remind him. He followed Kanesewah's size twelves to the rear driver's-side door of the missing car, where Sharon's tracks ended, then trailed them around what would have been the back of the car to the front passenger door, ending at the tread marks left by the missing car. This new woman was driving, with Kanesewah riding shotgun. He followed the tire tracks around the north side of the house and watched them trail off toward the blacktop of Highway 191. Then he walked past the front of the house and stood there. Judging by the drying mud left by the girl washing the car, and the look of these Firestone tracks running through it, they had at least eight or nine hours on him. He sighed and walked back to the Bronco.

After climbing in, he rubbed the thick fur of Ak'is' head, gave him a quick scratch behind the ears, and started the engine. Cranking the steering wheel hard to the right, he made a U-turn on the dirt street that brought him back down the dusty entry road. He slowed as he got to the end of it, put the Bronco in park, and got out with the engine running. Ak'is watched intently from the passenger seat as Arthur picked up the tracks quickly enough. They had made the turn north onto 191 as the now-dried mud had touched the pavement and then quickly vanished against the blacktop. Eight or nine hours. He remembered what he had told Agent Thorne about the hardball.

CHAPTER THIRTEEN

Leonard Kanesewah sat in the driver's seat, working the dial on the Delco radio, looking for a station that might stand out from the weaker ones he had already passed. The clock on the dash had just rolled to 5:36 a.m. when he finally landed on KUWX.

The University of Wyoming station was just winding up its weather report. "Watch out for lows tonight in the high teens with snow totals ranging from around ten inches in the valley to three feet in the mountains. This early winter storm is really going to pack a wallop tonight, friends, but the snow should trail off by morning, with tomorrow's highs only getting to the midthirties, but the wind chill will make it feel like the midtwenties. Look for temps tomorrow night in the low twenties …"

He flicked off the radio. "Damn it!" He looked at the woman. "You sure you packed all the shit I told you to?"

She returned fire. "You packed it all in the trunk last night! You know it's all there!"

Sharon Nakai sat silent in the middle of the back seat,

watching them spar. She was grateful that his woman had not rebound her ankles with the nylon rope when they got back to the car. She would have liked to get the duct tape off her mouth, too—over time, the nauseating taste had gotten worse. With her hands tied behind her, she found it difficult to lean back against the seat without further restricting her already-compromised circulation. Her fingers had been in an almost perpetual state of pins and needles ever since this nightmare began. All she could do now was keep flexing them to keep the numbness at bay.

"How much longer do you plan on keeping *her*?" the woman said, cutting a glance Sharon's way. "It doesn't even seem like we need her anymore, baby. There's no one even following us."

Kanesewah kept his eyes on the mountains rising high in the middle distance. "If things go like I planned," he said, "we'll be getting rid of her around Glacier. She'll be no use to us once we get that far." He stared out the windshield. "It'll be spring thaw before anyone finds her."

The cold lump in the pit of Sharon's stomach grew heavier. She tried to swallow as her eyes darted from Kanesewah to his woman, then back to him. She tried to control her breathing, but the quick, shallow snuffling through her nostrils only made him grin. *Stay calm*, she told herself. *They've already freed your legs. Just keep your head and wait for your chance.*

"What kind of food did you pack?" His tone was curt.

"Some peanut-butter granola bars, trail mix, a few cans of beans, and some bags of chips," she rattled off confidently. "And a couple gallons of water."

"Great," he said. "Faggot food, fart food, and fucking *chips*. I ate better on the rez, and that isn't saying much."

"Well, I didn't have a lot of time to buy shit," the woman argued. "I had to move fast and take what I could grab from my place."

"Whatever," he said, his empty gaze still on the distant mountains. "Get me a peanut-butter bar."

The woman pulled the keys from the ignition, got out of the car, and walked back to the trunk. Sharon heard the keys rattle against the primered metal and the trunk lid rock hard against its springs. After rummaging a bit, the woman slammed the trunk lid, removed the keys, and got back in the car. She shoved the keys back in the ignition, opened the box, and handed Kanesewah a bottle of water and a pack of granola bars, and set two other bottles of water on the front seat. Kanesewah grimaced but took the bars. Sitting angled in the passenger seat, she pulled another package out and set the open box between them on the front seat.

"You that thirsty?" Kanesewah said.

"I got a bottle for her, asshole. If you want to keep her alive, she's gotta at least drink some fucking water."

Kanesewah turned his attention back to his granola bars.

Sharon looked on, her growling stomach reminding her that she had not eaten since breakfast the day before. But more than anything, she wanted some water from that unopened bottle in the front seat. She thought of Arthur. Where was he? Would he come after her? *Of course he'll come after you*, she told herself, and shook off the thought. He was already looking. She could feel it. Or maybe it was just hope. The question now was, could he find her before they reached Glacier National Park and her time ran out?

Her thoughts were broken by the woman's voice, asking if she wanted a granola bar. She nodded apprehensively and looked down at the duct tape. The woman reached over the seat, got a fingernail under one corner of the tape, and began to peel it away. The intermittent tugging felt as though a layer of skin were coming off with the tape. Sharon tried to push it with her tongue, but it didn't help. Once her mouth was partially uncovered, she sucked in her first full breath in eighteen hours. It felt good, and it reinforced the reality that she was still alive. When the woman had worked the tape to the opposite side of her face, she gave it a swift jerk and ripped it free.

After the sting subsided, Sharon worked her lips and jaw as if trying them out for the first time. Then she said, "My hands, too?"

Kanesewah shook his head and laughed. "What do you think we are, fucking stupid?" He motioned with a jerk of his chin. "Give her some water first and then feed her.

The woman twisted off the plastic cap and put the bottle to Sharon's lips. She glugged down half of it before the woman jerked it away, put the cap back on, and set it on the seat, saying, "Jesus!" Then the woman tore open another pack of granola bars and stuck one in Sharon's mouth. The dry bar may as well have been chicken Parmesan, it tasted so good.

When both bars were gone, the woman tossed the wrapper on the front floorboard with the others, held the bottle to Sharon's mouth again, and watched her guzzle the rest. Then she tossed the empty bottle on the floorboard and pulled the roll of duct tape out of the glove compartment.

"Please don't," Sharon said. "I promise I won't … I—I just can't have that on me again."

The woman looked at Kanesewah. He seemed to consider the request, then nodded, and she put the tape back in the glove compartment. She closed the box of peanut butter bars and stashed them with the duct tape and the atlas.

"We need to look for a new car," Kanesewah said. "A guy I knew told me once that if you're ever on the run not to keep a car or stay in any one place for more than two days."

"But this is my car," the woman said. "No one knows shit about this car. Hell, no one even knows about *me*, let alone that I'm with you!"

"This isn't a discussion," he said. "We're not taking a vote here. We're gonna dump this pile of shit and pick up another car tomorrow, and that's the end of it. Jackson's gonna be our best shot for that. Then we keep moving north."

"But this car cost me three grand!"

Kanesewah's stare was mean and true. He didn't have to say a word.

The woman's eyes moved away from his. Sharon could see in her face that she was in way over her head. She had better learn to get with the program and not give him any reason to mistrust her. Maybe that would keep her alive. "Sure, baby, sure. Whatever you say."

He opened the car door and got out, then leaned back in. "You'd better get some sleep. You're driving tonight." He looked at Sharon. "I wanna get to know our friend here a little better."

The woman said nothing as he closed the car door—just folded her arms, hunkered down in the front seat, and turned toward the window.

Kanesewah opened the rear driver's-side door. "Get out," he

said, grabbing Sharon's left arm and hauling her from the car, then kicking the door shut. While he held Sharon in a bruising grip, she struggled with her high heels on the uneven earth. He jerked her close and murmured in a calm, clear voice, "Don't pull any shit or I swear I'll kill you right here." He let go of her arm and grabbed the black rope that dangled from her tied wrists, shoved her forward. "Now, walk."

Sharon felt the cold, hard muzzle of the .38 revolver in the small of her back as they moved deeper in among the cottonwoods. Beyond the trees, she heard the creek, swollen from the recent rains running off the mountains. The twilit forest was coming into focus. Another half hour, and it would be full daylight. The heels of her shoes punched into the ground, her ankles wobbling precariously as she walked through the short grass and over the sprays of twigs that had fallen from the cottonwoods. When they reached a place to his liking, Kanesewah stopped and told her to sit. She sat.

"I'll be right back," he said, dropping the length of rope and holding up the gun. "Remember, you run, you die."

Sharon watched him move toward the creek, tuck the .38 into the back of his waistband, and take up the typical male stance to relieve himself. In the gray predawn, she could begin to make out the boisterous creek waters tumbling over rocks that would soon be glazed in a growing sheath of ice. She savored each breath of fresh mountain air as if it might be her last. The thought made her swallow hard. Any other time, this would be a welcoming place of serenity. Not now.

Kanesewah returned from the creek and sat down facing her with his back resting against another tree. Reaching into a jacket pocket, he took a cigarette from the pack and lit up. With a flick of his wrist, the lighter snapped shut, and he stuffed the hard pack back into his jacket. He sat for a long moment looking at her. Then, pointing at her with the cigarette, he said, "You believe me when I say I will kill you, don't you?"

"Why shouldn't I, Leonard?" she replied. *Get him talking. Get him talking and keep him talking. Even Ted Bundy couldn't shut up once he started.* Her knowing his name had startled him. She could see it. "You're the one holding the gun. And I have no reason to think you're a liar."

Kanesewah stared intently, then gave a little barking laugh and bobbed his head in agreement. "How did you know my name?"

"The car speakers," she replied. "I heard everything about you."

He took a drag off his cigarette and let smoke trail from his mouth. "I don't really care anymore. I've got nothing left to lose."

Sharon motioned with her head toward the car. "Does *she* know that?"

He paused. "Gloria? She knows what I tell her."

"I ask only because I want to get your story correctly." She had cast the line and was hoping for a nibble. And she got one.

"You want to interview *me*?" His gaze was skeptical.

"Only if you want me to," Sharon said. "I'm sure people would be interested in knowing why you killed that girl and all those others, including my cameraman, and kidnapped me."

Now she had his attention. "What girl?"

Sharon took a breath. "Renée Braun. Told you, I heard it all through the speakers."

Kanesewah's eyes narrowed in such a way that they filled the serene morning air with the palpable feeling of something sinister working through his dark mind. After a long moment, he finally said, "You think doing this will keep you alive?"

"I'm a reporter," Sharon said. "This is what I do. Whether it keeps me alive is entirely up to you." She paused for effect, then asked, "Why did you kill Renée Braun?"

He grinned. "Because nobody else was around when I found her by the lake. She was just standing there, like a gift … staring at the water." The grin broadened. "She was mine for the taking."

Sharon nodded. "I see. And did you enjoy killing her?"

"Enjoy it?" he said. "It was …" He paused as if letting his mind search for just the right word. "… intoxicating." His eyes suddenly locked with Sharon's. "You ever killed anything?"

"Of course, not," Sharon replied.

"I didn't think so." He adjusted his position on the leaf-covered ground and leaned forward slightly, as if to tell her a secret. "You wanna know how I killed her, don't you? How I took my time with her … made her beg. Just like I will with you."

Sharon tried to swallow away the dryness that lined her throat. She felt as though she was facing Death without so much as a chessboard between them. "Start from wherever you like."

Kanesewah shrugged and leaned back against the tree. "She was so scared, it was beautiful," he said. "Lying there under me, whimpering and begging me to stop, as if that was ever going to happen." He took a drag off the cigarette. "When I put my knife against her throat, she shut up. After a while, it just became nauseating, all that pleading. The edge of my blade was so sharp that it left little red lines of blood across her throat after

I removed it. Then, just when she thought I wasn't going to kill her, I drove the blade into her belly." Cigarette smoke belched from his mouth as he talked. "She gasped, and her eyes got *really* wide. Stupid fucking kids—they think everything bad is going to happen to everyone else but them." He glanced toward the car again. "Then I kept pulling it out and jamming it back in until she started choking on her own blood. It didn't take long before it filled her lungs." He sighed heavily. "It's extraordinary, watching someone's life just drain away."

"And then you buried her?" Sharon prodded.

He took a deeper drag off his cigarette and smiled. "Oh, no, no, no," he said. The smoke slithered like a snake's tongue from his mouth and drifted toward the morning sky. "I wasn't finished yet."

Sharon's brow creased.

"After cleaning her blood off my knife, I ripped open her sweater and blouse and laid her open to me. Then I sliced her bra so I could see those sweet tits … and then I tasted them." His eyes closed, basking in the memory. "Um-m-m. I had forgotten how sweet a sixteen-year-old could be. All full of hormones and promise." His grin revolted Sharon. "Then I got rid of those tiny shorts and …" He paused to take the pair of panties with a little white bow from his pants pocket. "These." He sniffed them again and watched the shudder run through Sharon's body. "She told me she was from Michigan. Man, there isn't anything sweeter than a Michigan cherry. And she tasted so exquisite on my tongue." Sharon watched his eyes cloud with desire as he laid out the rest of his story. "Her body was still warm when I entered her. And she took me willingly. Willingly and deep. While I was on top of her, she seemed to move with every motion of my body. As if we were one being, you know?"

Sharon nodded, trying to turn off the sickening image now playing on the screen of her mind. He took another puff and ground the rest of the cigarette into the damp leaf litter. "When we were finished, I dressed and then buried her. Laid her out in a way so that she could travel to the next life." He dug out his hard pack again, popped the lid, and shook one out. "I thought I heard some people, so I took off."

As Sharon watched him light up, she wished that Arthur had already found them. Dear God, where was he? Why wasn't he already here?

"When I was a kid on the rez," he continued, "we didn't have much. Us poor Indians, you know? My father was an alcoholic. He abandoned me and my mother when I was five years old. My mother said it was because he couldn't take the warrior's responsibility of providing for his family. I just thought he was weak." As he spoke, the ashes fell from the end of his cigarette onto his jacket. Ashes that he absently brushed it away. "My mother, she was a good woman in the beginning, but the loneliness and the responsibility got to her, too. She became something different. She started to sleep around and lost herself in the curse of alcohol. And when she drank, she would beat me. Hit me in the head, kick me. One time, she even pulled a kitchen knife on me. All sorts of anger would come out." He hung his head briefly and took a slower drag off his cigarette. "One day, while she was beating the shit out of me in another drunken rage, she told me she should have kept the afterbirth instead of the me." The smoke curled around his head as he spoke. "The next day, when she looked at me and saw what she'd done, she apologized and promised it would never happen again." He gave a heavy sigh. "But when she drank, it always happened again." He half snickered at a new memory. "You know, I never asked to be born, but I sure as hell heard every day why I shouldn't have been."

Sharon listened attentively to this devil in human form, carefully transferring away every dictated word onto the thumb drive of her reporter's mind. "I'm sure she loved you," Sharon said. "You were still her son."

"She couldn't have cared less," he replied flatly. "Most of the time, she just blamed me for my father leaving and how the rest of her life had turned out."

"But she was still your mother."

"She was a whore," he snapped. "Nothing but a drunken whore. Each week was a different man. Sometimes white, sometimes Mexican, sometimes Indian. She thought the only way to get ahead was to give it. But no man worth anything wants a drunk Indian with a kid to fuck up his life."

He stubbed out his cigarette before lighting the next in the chain. "You see, when my mother drank, she often smoked." Sharon watched his eyes through the wavering smoke. "One night, there was a fire. I made it look like she had fallen asleep after a drunken binge, and the whole place went up. Fire department just let it burn. No water out where we were, and there was no one they could save anyway."

"I see," Sharon said. "And what happened to that little boy?"

Kanesewah shrugged off the years that had followed, and spoke of being taken in by his mother's sister and her people, the White Mountain People. And when they couldn't handle him, how they dumped him off at some Christian mission school, thinking they would be able to curb his rebellious nature. "That was where I did as I was told until I was of age and was turned loose from the white man's school. Their god meant nothing to me. And once I was free of it, I roamed around, had odd jobs, and made enough money to hit the bars at night. That's when the need to hunt began."

"Hunt?" Sharon said.

He smiled. "Like the true hunter, you learn to separate the weak from the strong of the herd. One night, I found a girl in a place I never expected to be, but hey, your hunting ground changes when the prospects are slim."

"And what kind of place was this?" Sharon asked. The morning began to brighten, the sunrise contrasting with the dark story.

"Some sex shop in Phoenix. I don't recall the name. She was all glassy-eyed in the bondage section. Secretly, you're all into that *Fifty Shades* shit. Only most of you don't admit it. Anyway, I got her talking, and when she felt at ease with me, I offered to take her for a drink." He grinned. "Most women are oblivious, especially the young ones. They're always willing to talk with any guy that buys them a drink and flashes some cash. Long story short, once you've got them, the rest is easy. Some like to be choked. Some like to be abused. Some like to be tied up. And that's when it gets interesting. Because I've got this special rope I like to use—like what I used on you … but much more fun."

"And are you killing these women because they all, in some way, remind you of your mother?" Sharon prodded. "Or is there some other reason?"

Kanesewah paused to think about it. "Because they all need to be taught a lesson. Women are blessed creatures. You yourself should know this. You are meant to be the givers of life, not become degraded whores pandering for a handout." He tilted his head back against the cottonwood trunk and stared up through half-denuded branches at the bluing sky. "You know, when you're at that moment—that one final second before you watch the life disappear from their eyes—you realize that you have all the power. You get to decide who lives and who dies." His head cocked to the left. "And *how* they die." Pulling his legs up, he wrapped his arms around his knees, brought his eyes down to meet his captive's. "The Braun girl never even knew I was there. I pulled my knife and snuck up quietly behind her. My left hand was over her mouth before she even felt my blade against her throat."

Sharon heard the swallow that seemed to reverberate from her throat. "And do you always use a knife? Why not a gun?"

"Because a gun is for cowards," he replied. "A gun is for killing at a distance. There is no honor in that. A knife—that makes it personal, honorable. You get to watch them as they die."

CHAPTER FOURTEEN

Arthur kept his eyes on the advancing road while his fingers worked the Bronco's dial away from its usual home, KNDN radio, "all Navajo all the time." Ak'is sat in the passenger seat, soaking up the warmth pumped out by the Bronco's heater. Tongue protruding slightly from the front of his open mouth, he watched the rain, perking his ears every time lightning flashed or thunder rolled. Arthur settled on KCYN and the *Canyon Country Morning Show.* Phil Mueller was warning his listeners about the heavy line of thunderstorms pushing its way east across the windswept lands of the Goblin Valley, into Moab. The storm line had taken the shape of a large bow echo coming from Salt Lake City, curving at its farthest point past Moab, and continuing down toward Bluff, where Arthur had entered the storm. He felt as though it had been tracking him every step of the way and was now beginning to intensify as he left Blanding.

Clicking off the radio, he switched on his CB and turned the knob to WX. He tapped the button and scanned for the closest NOAA signal. As soon as he heard the Stephen Hawking–sounding voice from the small speaker, he stopped the scan. With the voice of NOAA keeping him company, he weighed the idea of calling Jake Bilagody and telling him what he had learned at the house where Billy found the gray beater Impala with the rolled-down windows. Then he thought about how he was going to figure out where Kanesewah was heading, and how he would go about finding him. But mainly, he thought about Sharon. Did she know he was coming for her? He wondered whether she had been harmed. And he wondered at what point Kanesewah would decide that he didn't need her anymore … or whether he already had.

He pushed through that thought as he stared out the windshield at the successive curtains of wind-driven rain. His hands gripped the wheel, fighting the hard gusts that pushed the Bronco toward the right shoulder and then sheared abruptly, causing him to steer left over the dividing line. If it got any worse, he would have to pull off somewhere and sit it out. But that would only increase the distance between him and Kanesewah—and bring him that much closer to running out of time. The decision had already been made for him. There was no stopping, no turning back.

He pushed past the reddish-khaki shores of Recapture Reservoir, now darkened by the heavy rain, and skirted around South Peak, then swung past the Abajo Mountains and entered Monticello. Crossing the intersection of Highways 191 and 491 at a green light, he turned into the parking lot just past the TacoTime sign that stood above a white propane tank and parked in an open spot. After telling Ak'is to wait in the truck, he pulled up the collar of his denim jacket and got out. He jogged past the pumps and the smell of gasoline and went inside the Shell station.

After a brief stop to void his bladder, he grabbed a square bottle of Pure Leaf tea for himself and a bottle of water for his furry partner, along with two packages of beef sticks. Back in the Bronco, he opened the bottle of water. Ak'is sat patiently, eyes riveted on Arthur's hands. He watched Arthur crack open the tea and drink a mouthful before capping the bottle and setting it in the center console's cup holder. The predator eyes stayed on Arthur as he opened the console and pulled out a collapsible silicone water bowl. It had been Sharon's idea—she hated the cheap plastic collapsible cups because they always broke. He popped it open and poured water into it. Ak'is lapped it dry before returning his attention to the not-yet-visible beef sticks. Arthur tore open a package and pulled two sticks from it. He bit down on one and gave the other to Ak'is. He hadn't finished chewing his stick when Ak'is was staring at him again, waiting for more. Arthur smiled, rubbed the big furry head, and gave him another half stick.

After devouring the rest of the processed beef, he tossed the empty packages into the truck's console, along with the collapsible bowl, and turned the key. The wipers flung the falling rain clear as he checked the gas gauge. He had enough to make it to Moab, so he rolled back out onto 191 and continued north. Noticing a small row of semis parked in a larger lot north of the station, he wondered whether Billy had ever parked here on one of his runs. He remembered hunting near here, at Range Creek in the Blue Mountains, long before he met Sharon, before Waldo

Wilcox sold the land to the State of Utah. He had liked being in this part of the Tavaputs Plateau, moving silently through its thick forests in search of a browsing muley buck. You had to catch them at night or just before dawn, he remembered, because they preferred to shelter during the day.

He passed the Canyon Motor Inn—just a few cars in the lot—and the Bureau of Land Management field office. He was looking for somewhere Ak'is could empty his bladder and whatever else needed emptying, and the BLM lot seemed a little too civilized. He would have to find a more suitable place out of town.

He drove on through the steady rain, up the gradual incline out of town, where the hillside rose to his left and fell away on the right, down to the now drenched valley floor. Where the road crested, he crossed the southbound lane and pulled over by the city of Monticello's hamburger-shaped wooden THANK YOU, COME AGAIN! sign. He let Ak'is out. The wolf-dog darted past the sign, sniffed at a scrawny patch of snakeweed, and hiked his leg, then moved on with his nose hovering just above the ground. He soon found a suitable spot to arch his back and make a deposit, then galloped back to the truck and jumped in.

Arthur shook his head. Nothing worse than the smell of wet dog. Reaching into the back seat for a blanket, he wiped the animal down and tossed the blanket back onto the back seat. He told Ak'is to follow it, and the animal curled up on the blanket and lay down.

"What do you think?" Arthur asked. "Think I should give Jake a call?"

The dog just stared up from his relaxed position on the seat and licked his lips, as if savoring the lingering taste of beef stick.

Arthur thought more about his idea as the truck idled in the rain. If he told Jake about the house, Jake would have to inform Special Agent Thorne. Soon after, Thorne would have his suits all over that house, thick as the flies in the kitchen. And he couldn't forget about the rain. He remembered the preceding wind that had blown in with the thunderheads as they trampled like a herd of bison across the darkening sky, bringing with them the early smell of rain. But what if it hadn't rained at the house? Would the G-men be able to pick up the sign he had found? Probably not. But if they did, Thorne would surely realize that his suspect wasn't heading south, but north to God knew where. Arthur grinned. He would pay to be the fly on that wall when Thorne told his superior of that new revelation.

But where *was* Kanesewah heading, and for what reason? Arthur pondered that for a moment. If he were the fugitive, he would stick to the smaller roads and use the interstate only when there was no other way to move. And since he was probably changing cars more frequently now, he would be harder to track. To find Sharon, he would have to think like Kanesewah. Did the man have any family in the north? Did he have any pals or old girlfriends who might live up here? *Oh, hell with it.* He fished his cell phone out of his jacket pocket, brought up his contacts list, and tapped Jake's office number in Shiprock. It took an extra moment for his cell phone to be rerouted to the phone on Jake's desk, but soon he heard it ringing. Three rings later, the acting chief of the Navajo Nation Police picked up.

"Bilagody."

"Jake? It's Arthur."

"How's the moose hunting going?"

"Not too bad," Arthur said. "I found Kanesewah's car. It's parked behind a tan cinder-block house just across the Utah border, off One Ninety-One."

"Any sign of Sharon?"

"They were already gone by the time I got there. But I found three sets of tracks, including Sharon's. Kanesewah's got another woman with him. She's probably just a little over five feet tall and between one fifteen and one thirty, judging by the size and depth of the footprint."

Jake grunted. "Thorne's gonna be pissed when I tell him his boy fled north."

Arthur disregarded the statement. "Does Kanesewah have any reason to head north? Any family you know of?"

Jake said nothing for a moment. "None I can recall hearing about."

"Can you buy me some time with Thorne?" Arthur asked. "Sharon's tracks prove she's alive."

Jake groaned. "Now, you know Thorne would have my badge if I withheld information."

"Yeah," Arthur said, "and?"

"Don't give me that shit! What am I supposed to tell him if he asks me to my face? You want me to lie to a federal agent? The word 'obstruction' comes to mind."

"She's alive, Jake; that's what I know. Now, are you going to buy me some time or not?"

In the silence, Arthur could almost hear Jake weighing the possibilities, struggling with duty over conscience. Finally, conscience won out. "I'll give you eight hours, no more. Clock starts this minute."

"Thanks. I'll owe you one."

"You'll owe me a big fat one if I'm still around after all this and not under investigation. Lying to the FBI helped get that Illinois governor an extra five years, you know." Jake took a deep breath and let the weight of his chest push it out. "Besides, right now I've got a neighborhood search in progress for some yahoo that took a potshot at a Navajo Utility Authority employee today, so I figure I can do the dance steps with Thorne later."

"What?" Arthur said. "Where?"

"Up around Fort Defiance," Jake explained. "I've got men from two districts up there working with some Apache County Sheriff deputies and an FBI agent Thorne sent over."

"You have an idea who took the shot?" Arthur asked.

"Not sure yet, but they're working their way to a house we've been told a guy is holed up in. The Navajo Criminal Investigations team is on their way as backup, and the Fire Department is diverting traffic from the area. We don't know how much firepower this guy has got, so we're not taking chances. Jake returned his thought to the conversation at hand. "Like I said, you've got seven hours and fifty-eight minutes. After that, I call Thorne and piss him off." Arthur heard him chuckle. "And I think I'm gonna enjoy that."

CHAPTER FIFTEEN

Sharon Keonie Nakai shivered, but not from the cold of daybreak that fogged her breath in the air. It was because she sat across from a man for whom killing had become a kind of retribution, where each victim was specifically chosen to represent what he despised most. She had heard of his kind before. Some psychopaths were driven by a history of rejection from the opposite sex, while others were driven by a vengeance that had its basis in anger due to childhood abuse. But all of them seemed to have that balanced mix of charm and cunning and intimidation that coupled dangerously with a need to exert control over others. If anything, Leonard Kanesewah seemed to be all those wrapped up in one demented soul. Sharon tried to swallow but couldn't; her mouth was still too dry. She trembled noticeably, but regained her composure before he could take note of it.

She turned her thoughts to the woman, Gloria. Did he intend on keeping his promise, or was he beginning to see her as more of a liability than an asset? Their relationship seemed to be more physical than romantic, and maybe more than a little codependent. And codependence was odd for a man like him, but some serial killers, such as Robert Lee Yates, Gary Ridgway, and Dennis Rader, had been family men and active church members, and codependence never entered into their makeup. Gloria's view of their relationship seemed a bit more rose colored, while Kanesewah seemed to think of her as just a sexual outlet. Sharon had determined that he saw women as necessary yet personally insignificant.

"And why did you kill Oscar Hirada?" Sharon asked.

Kanesewah looked puzzled. "Who?"

"My cameraman," she said. "Why him?"

"I saw him looking at his phone. He saw me. He recognized me. End of story." He stood up and looked down at her.

"And do you really intend to kill me once you get around Glacier?"

He smiled and said nothing.

"But I'm your insurance," Sharon said. "The police, and by now the FBI, know you have me, and that could be used to your advantage."

Kanesewah lifted her off the ground by her upper arms and stood her in front of him. "You're forgetting some things," he said. "No one knows where we are or where we're going, so keeping you alive is really not important. You are breathing only because I allow it."

"Will you at least untie my hands? They're getting awfully numb."

Kanesewah thought for a moment, twirled her around and untied the rope. Then motioned toward the car with his head.

"Now, move. We need sleep before nightfall."

They said nothing more on their way back to the car. When they got there, Gloria awoke and gave Sharon a resentful glare. "I'm cold," she said in a childlike voice.

"Hope you brought some blankets, because we're not wasting gas keeping this heap running all day with the heat on. Don't need anyone spotting exhaust from these trees."

"They're in the trunk."

Kanesewah grabbed the keys, took three blankets from the trunk, and got back into the driver's seat. He kept one and gave his girlfriend two. "Remember," he said to Sharon, holding up the revolver. "I sleep light. If you try to leave this car, I will kill you."

Sharon nodded. Gloria smiled. Kanesewah covered himself with a blanket, gun in hand beneath it, leaned against the door, and closed his eyes. Gloria had Sharon lie down as before, then unfurled a blanket and covered her. That task completed, she slid across the front seat and snuggled against Kanesewah's warmth and closed her eyes. He seemed to pay her no mind.

Sharon felt the blanket slowly beginning to retain her body heat, and her eyelids grew heavy. Arthur's face materialized on the walls of her mind, transporting her back to the day they first met at the Chaco ruins. That vision was short-lived and soon dissolved into the anguished look on his face after watching them pull the lifeless little boy from her body.

Her thoughts dredged up a mix of sorrow, rage, and self-doubt that she hadn't allowed herself to feel since they took her child, washed and swaddled him, and placed his lifeless body in her arms. And she remembered cradling him for two hours and not letting them take him. And she remembered Arthur breaking down and leaving the room as she rocked him gently in her arms, singing him soft Navajo lullabies until she allowed them to gently take him away. When Arthur returned, they did not speak. They just held each other as the wave of grief crashed over them.

She remembered coming home to an empty nursery, remembered locking its door securely against her sorrow. She remembered the months that followed as she lay in bed and did nothing but try to wrap her mind around the unthinkable reality of it all. And even more months that had to pass before she regained the will even to venture outside and once again feel the warmth of the sun against her face. And the dark year that passed before she went back to work.

She could still see the quickly averted looks from those who couldn't find the words to speak to her, and the uninvited questions from others who brought it all back. The few whom she counted as friends had held her as if they understood, but even they couldn't fathom the loss. Sharon moved a trembling hand from under the blanket and wiped away the silent tears. Perhaps, if she survived this ordeal, they could once again hold the possibility of a child within their grasp. A new way. A new life. A new beginning.

CHAPTER SIXTEEN

Eight hours, Arthur reflected. Four hundred eighty minutes. Twenty-eight thousand, eight hundred seconds. He took a deep breath and let it out. With more than a thousand miles of mountainous terrain ahead of him, it still didn't seem like enough time. He had begun to feel the heavy weight of his role in this game he was being forced to play. A game that he must engage in fully, because the grand prize was Sharon's life.

He began moving through the maze of possibilities, trying to pursue each forking pathway to its logical end. Kanesewah was running. Keeping out of sight and moving with purpose, making his way north to some unknown destination. *Had he already reached wherever he was going, and taken refuge? Or had he been smarter than the average runner and succeeded at misdirecting everyone?* Arthur rocked his tired head back on his broad shoulders. If he had learned anything about the patterns of runners during his years of tracking them across the desert, it was that he should continue north until his gut told him differently. And he had always trusted his gut. Just as he had that time when he discovered six UDAs packed like sardines beneath the rubber mat in the cutout bed of a pickup truck. He had chuckled at the sight of their astonished faces as the mat was peeled away from their claustrophobic hiding place.

He filled the Bronco's tank in Moab and crossed the Colorado River at Lion's Park. Driving over the split highway bridge that spanned the roiling green water, he saw the Moab Canyons Pathway walking bridge off to his right. Normally, it was alive with vacationers and hikers, but on this rain-soaked late afternoon, it stood empty. Back on solid land, he followed the highway's gradual turn past the tall, reddish canyon cliff on his right and the campground on his left, then the small power substation and the western entrance to Arches National Park.

His parents had taken him there when he was fifteen. Arches Scenic Drive snaked past majestic towers and into the vast primeval splendor of petrified sand dunes, where dusty arteries had been carved into the red rock by fifty million years of rain. He remembered gazing at Balanced Rock and marveling at its harmony. If only he could achieve such balance.

He remembered almost losing the sight in his right eye after aiming his camera into the opening of North Window. The optical magnification of the sun through the lens had temporarily blinded him, scaring his young body into trembling as he managed to wander through the blurred surroundings to a place where he could sit down and whisper his prayers. After a short time, the Sun Father answered his earnest prayers, and his vision slowly returned. He had vowed then and there never to look at Jóhonaa'éí again while he was making his journey across the sky. He never told his parents.

Ten miles out of Moab, he passed a resort with its log-cabin souvenir shop, campground, mock-up schoolhouse, and gas station. They had even thrown in two spurious-looking Native American tepees for good measure. Still, he had to hand it to the creators of this whole tawdry spectacle for backdropping it against a magnificent red sandstone butte.

Twenty silent minutes later, the winding snake of Highway 191 met with Interstate 70 at Crescent Junction. Ak'is, apparently tired of the rain and wind, decided to hop into the back seat and curl up for a nap as they drove on. Thinking had become wearisome for Arthur, so he tried not to think. His brain was tired of pondering, tired of concocting, tired of imagining scenarios that hadn't played out anywhere but in his exhausted mind. Letting go of his frenetic thoughts, he pushed on through the heavy rain.

Now, as the Bronco rolled beneath the expansive bridge deck of I-70, Arthur spun the steering wheel and felt the tires drop off the end of the pavement. He guided the truck into a spot in the dirt lot of Papa Joe's Stop & Go to consider his options. Pulling a tattered road atlas from the overhead shelf above the windshield, he propped it open against the steering wheel. He quickly located the page assigned to Utah and pored over it, noting every road, every path of escape.

Kanesewah would have thought twice before heading east into Colorado, because that would mean staying on the busy interstate and increasing his odds of being spotted by any tourist, long-haul trucker, or watchful state trooper he might stumble across. The only way to keep a low profile would have been to head west a few miles and get himself back on 191 just past Green River. After that, it would be easy enough to roll past

Elliot Mesa and Mount Elliot and get across the Price River. From there, Arthur followed his finger north through Helper, deeper into the mountains. It would be another almost three hours to Flaming Gorge. Once Kanesewah passed the ranger station at Dutch John, he could easily wind his way deeper into Wyoming. He nodded to himself. That was the route he would use if he were on the run.

Arthur closed the atlas and shoved it back onto the overhead shelf, getting the eye from Ak'is the entire time. It was the look that meant the waves in his bladder were cresting. Arthur let him out to water the mud and then hit the head in the Stop & Go before pointing the Bronco back onto the blacktop and up the I-70 entrance ramp. He would make Rock Springs, Wyoming, in about four hours.

As the rain beat steadily on the roof and hood, he found himself slipping into past mornings on the mesa, with Sharon lying beside him while the rain tapped out its rhythm on the ribbed steel roof. More times than not, he would wake to the tinkling of her wind chimes in the morning breeze. In summer, it meant that the hot, dry winds had made their way east across the high desert to White Mesa. In the fall, however, it represented the cool, bracing air that crept in and heightened the sweet scent of the black and silver sage surrounding their home.

He would turn his attention past the wafting curtains to be greeted by the clear, bright azure sky that often canopied their corner of the world. Sometimes, framed like a moving portrait in one of the windows, a pair of red-tailed hawks could be seen floating effortlessly on the wind in the near distance. He would watch them sail, their wings spread in enviable freedom, before they spiraled out of sight. Then he would roll onto his left side, prop his head in his hand, and gaze at the sleeping face of his wife. Sometimes, a lock of black hair would have fallen across her face during the night and come to rest near the corner of her mouth. As he'd watch her sleep, a soft breath might lift the errant lock into mystical flight, then let it float down and fall gently back into place.

Grudgingly, he would roll back over to look at the time on the docking station. Ever since building their house on the mesa, one of his private joys had been to rise while darkness still covered the high desert, dress comfortably, and pad quietly downstairs to make a pot of coffee. He would shrug on his long Pendleton coat and go out into the morning twilight, his hands warming against his coffee mug.

He had his favorite spot, too: a long ledge of sandstone that curved away from him and disappeared down the canyon wall at the end of the mesa. There he would sit, overlooking the canyon floor, his back against the sloping wall behind him, the mug of coffee warming his hands, and wait. Wait for the tranquil silence to be given life while the sun climbed over Hooded Mesa's six-thousand-foot spine and spilled its light as if molten gold were being poured from a crucible into the canyon before him. Sometimes, the cry of a hawk would echo on the dawn breeze. He would then glance toward Spirit Lake and watch the newborn light dance on its shimmering surface, turning it into a glistening mirror on the canyon floor. Then, as the land began to come awake, he would stand as his father had taught him, facing east, eyes on the horizon, and slowly turn clockwise until he had completed a full circle.

"This is who I am," he would say aloud. "This is who I am."

He also remembered those rare mornings when Sharon would join him. He would speak the early morning blessing that told of how the mountains were their spiritual home and how, in the middle of this home, would be a warm fire. Of how thoughts would be good and plans would be made. Of how life would be blessed in this home where hope resided and where, together, they would sing as the morning unfolded.

Arthur's mind quickly jumped back into reality when the large green 191 exit sign loomed above the interstate ahead. As he peeled off from the superhighway, his body began to feel the toll from the early start to his day. And if that weren't enough, the drag of the afternoon tugged relentlessly at his tired, overworked mind. Add in the melancholy of unrelenting rain, and the choice became clear: at Rock Springs, he would pull off for some welcome shut-eye.

Unless he found that he couldn't sleep. Then he would find the biggest pot of coffee he could, drain it, and keep going, hoping that his calculating guesswork had not been flawed.

CHAPTER SEVENTEEN

The snow had been falling steadily for the past two hours, covering Jackson Hole with an almost Thomas Kinkade–like glow. Leonard Kanesewah drove the Buick slowly past the Million Dollar Cowboy Bar in all its garish electrified splendor. It was just after midnight. Gloria was staring out at the glowing marquee and the crimson-outlined saddle bronc and rider balanced precariously on the rooftop.

Sharon Nakai scanned the crowd of pedestrians for a familiar face, not knowing what she would do if she were to find one, but hoping nonetheless. Recognizing no one, she gazed out her side window and watched helplessly as the happy, laughing crowds carried on, blithely unaware of their presence.

Kanesewah's eyes, however, were busy roaming the crowded street, searching for the next vehicle for the final leg of their journey. It was somewhere in this town, among the rustic-looking restaurants, art galleries, and boutique shops of North Cache Street. The black facade and white-trimmed windows of the Anvil Hotel seemed to catch his eye, and the Buick slowed to a crawl as they passed. But nothing in the parking lot interested him, so he continued up Cache Street.

Sharon sat quietly in the back seat, remembering her college days, when she and a few of her friends had driven up to Jackson for a long weekend away from their New Mexico State University studies. They spent their days hiking the trails of the Tetons, and their evenings in the bar, shooting pool on any of the four red-felted tables while rebuffing thinly veiled attempts at conversation from drunken boys and horny middle-aged men. Funny, she thought, the kinds of things you thought about when trying to control the fear and focus your reeling mind.

Kanesewah tapped the brakes and turned in between the twin stone pillars of the Wolf Moon Inn. Moving slowly past the parked cars, he took the alley exit at the end of the first building, circled around, and turned south on Cache again. After circumnavigating the town square, he headed north again, back to the Wolf Moon's crowded parking lot. Something had caught his eye.

A Jackson police car pulled onto the crowded street from its blind under a darkened gas station portico. Sharon saw Kanesewah stiffen and his hands tighten on the steering wheel.

"Don't even think about it," he warned, peering into the rearview mirror at Sharon.

She watched in nervous silence as the police car drove slowly past, saw it blend into the crowd of cars and people behind them and vanish just as quickly as it had appeared. Her heart sank. Not so much as a glance from the officer behind the wheel. They may as well be invisible.

Kanesewah rolled into the Wolf Moon's parking lot again, toward the two-story block of rooms in back. He was eyeing a mocha-colored newer-model GMC Yukon with Minnesota plates. It sat high enough to be four-wheel drive, but in the snowy night, he couldn't be sure. He parked the Buick in an empty space across from the Yukon, turned off the headlights, and put it in park with the engine idling. He adjusted the rearview mirror to keep a watchful eye on the motel office behind them and to the right.

"What do we do now?" Gloria asked.

"We wait," he replied.

Gloria turned in the front seat, rested her left thigh against the seat back, and glanced at Sharon before staring out the windshield. No one spoke. Sharon, too, was looking out the windshield at the GMC, hoping it wasn't some vacationing senior citizen. If she were lotto-winner lucky, it would be an off-duty cop on some well-deserved R&R, and this nightmare would be over when Kanesewah tried to carjack him. Either way, her situation was about to change. But *how* it might change remained to be seen.

A few minutes into their vigil, a figure stepped out of a ground-floor motel room across from them—a tall man, wearing a shearling leather coat and dark cowboy hat. She watched as he stepped away from the weak light of the doorway and strode toward the mocha GMC. He stopped briefly in front of it to light a cigarette, then continued past it through the parking lot and toward the motel office. He paused outside the office door, beside a large smokers' receptacle resembling a chess pawn, and took a drag from his cigarette. Sharon breathed a quiet sigh of relief as the man finally crushed his cigarette on the pavement, ignoring the receptacle, and went inside the motel office.

More quiet time passed before another motel door opened. This time, it was a room on the second floor, near the left end of the long balcony, making it difficult to see the shadowy figure. She watched intently as the silhouette of a medium-size man walked away from the room and along the balcony to the stairs at the end. When he came down to the parking lot, she could see he was wearing a forest-green wool rancher's coat and a dark ball cap. He fumbled with something he took from one of his coat pockets, and the lights of the GMC blinked twice, accompanied by two brief chirps from the alarm. The man opened the driver's door and leaned in as if searching for something.

"Keep an eye on her," Kanesewah said, getting out of the car.

Gloria rested the .38 on the top of the seat back, pointed at Sharon. Sharon stared at it, then into the woman's eyes.

"How long have you been with him?" Sharon asked.

Gloria snorted. "Why? We girlfriends now or something? You want to paint our toenails later?"

"Just curious."

Gloria looked briefly behind her, through the snowflakes melting as they hit the warm windshield, at Kanesewah walking toward the Yukon and its unsuspecting owner. She turned her attention back to Sharon as Kanesewah stopped the man, produced a cigarette, and said something.

"Eight years."

"That's a long time," Sharon said. "And he hasn't asked you to marry him?"

Gloria smirked. "Leonard isn't the marrying kind. He's the fuck-you-hard kind.

"Then why do you stay with him?" The man produced a lighter and struck a flame. "He doesn't seem to treat you very well."

The first drip of doubt.

Gloria's irritation manifested quickly. "Shut up!" she barked. "He's good to me. You don't know a fucking thing about him! Sure, he's rough sometimes, but he's good to me."

Sharon measured out another drip.

"I just meant that I've known a lot of women whose husbands or boyfriends have treated them badly, and it never gets any better. They never change or they never commit."

Gloria craned her neck around toward the GMC and saw no one. Her eyes searched the parking lot before she answered. "Just shut the hell up, will you? You don't know a fucking thing!" The figure of a large man emerged from the shadows at the left end of the two-story inn. The long hair blowing in the snowy breeze told her it was Kanesewah, and that seemed to calm her anxiety. More snowflakes self-destructed on the warm windshield, running together to form droplets of water. "Once we get to Canada," she said, turning back to Sharon, "we're going to start a better life together."

Sharon said, "Is that what he promised you?"

Another measured dose.

"You don't know him," Gloria repeated, keeping the barrel of the revolver across the top of the seat back. "You don't know shit, Miss all-high-and-mighty TV Girl. He loves me."

"I didn't mean to upset you."

Drip.

"Shut up, I said. Just stop talking!"

Kanesewah opened the door and got in.

"I'm gonna pull up next to the GMC. You get the shit from the trunk, and I'll move her. And be quick about it. We can't afford to waste time."

"Sure, baby," Gloria said, handing over the .38 to Kanesewah.

Sharon had watched it all unfold during her conversation with Gloria. It was all she could do to keep her poker face on. After the man had lit the stranger's cigarette, she saw Kanesewah whip his left arm around the man's left shoulder as he stepped away, his large hand covering the man's mouth and nose, stifling any chance to scream. The man had struggled briefly while Kanesewah pulled something from his coat pocket and thrust it repeatedly into the man's torso. After the fourth thrust, the man's body wilted and Kanesewah hurriedly dragged him into the shadows of the motel. Sharon concluded that what was now in Kanesewah's coat pocket was either a bloodied switchblade or one of those folding knives that opened with just the flick of a thumb. And if they were indeed heading to Canada, she would have to use every moment alone with Gloria, no matter how brief, to drip more water on her newly planted seeds of doubt. Seeds that she hoped would grow into an impenetrable hedge of mistrust.

CHAPTER EIGHTEEN

Ak'is lay sprawled out on the thin pile carpet of Arthur's motel room at the Rock Springs Inn, twitching and dreaming about something worth chasing, his muffled barks coinciding with the excitement of the chase. Initially, he had taken up his position facing the locked and chained door, with the unwavering determination of a military honor guard, but after an hour or so, his eyelids had grown heavy and his body lost its battle with sleep.

In sharp contrast, Arthur's slumber had been uneasy, fraught with images of Sharon on their wedding day, which tumbled seamlessly into her broadcasting a live shot on television, which springboarded into a flashing kaleidoscope of pictures framing her different smiles throughout their ten years together. These flickering vignettes culminated in his distraught mind in a short film of Sharon's surprise meeting with Ak'is the day Arthur brought him to the mesa. His male logic had been bolstering his resolve on the drive back, reassuring him that it was better to ask for forgiveness than for permission. Stupid advice, he thought, and obviously conceived by someone who was single or soon would be.

Arthur remembered the uneasiness in his stomach, and the shocked look on her face when he had opened the door of the Bronco, and a huge, furry black carnivore jumped out in one fluid motion, catching her completely off guard. After a few hours of verbal confrontation, the kind that women seemed to master before the age of ten, she agreed to live with her husband's newfound companion, through a mutual understanding. *"He doesn't care about me anyway,"* she had said. *"He's your dog."* She crossed her arms. *"You're the one who saved him from that cage. Brothers to the end now, I suppose. We will simply have to agree to tolerate each other, I guess."*

Arthur's mind began to make the fast climb from its pit of memories as soft growls and sporadic huffs interrupted his recollections. The sounds Ak'is made while lost in deep sleep always made him smile. He sat up and rubbed his face and looked over the side of the queen-size bed. The room was dark, but light had managed to reach under the bottom of the door from the hallway on the other side, giving him enough illumination to see Ak'is' legs twitching and his large paws moving as if he were chasing elusive prey. Just then, Arthur's cell phone shattered the quiet with its familiar buzzing hum. The red glow of the room's clock radio declared it was 8:46 p.m. when he picked up the cell phone and recognized the name and number on its glowing screen. He tapped ACCEPT.

"Yá'át'ééh," Arthur said.

"Yá'át'ééh," Jake repeated. "Sorry to call so late, but I just got the chance."

"Not a problem," Arthur replied. "What's up?"

"Where the hell are you?"

"Wyoming," Arthur said, "Rock Springs."

"Well, I gave you your eight hours, and it cost me my backside getting reamed a new one by Agent Thorne a couple of hours ago."

Arthur gave a wry grin. "How pissed was he?"

"Pissed enough to think I had been holding out on him. Started spouting all kinds of buffalo crap at me. Then I tried explaining that you were simply playing a hunch and had done the right thing by contacting me. Not that he believed that. In fact, all it did was let him know that you're actively looking for Kanesewah." He paused. "If you get in his way, he's gonna arrest you for interfering in a federal investigation."

Arthur rubbed his face again. "I'm shaking in my boots. What he's got in the works?"

"He dispatched a detail to Utah to check out the house you found. By now they're probably bothering the neighbors with all their floodlights and scurrying around like red ants devouring a frog. I told him you also mentioned there was evidence of another woman besides Sharon in the mix. He's got his people going through everything pertaining to Kanesewah to see if they can figure out anything that might give them a name." Bilagody paused again. "What led you to Rock Springs?"

"Like you said, a hunch." Arthur threw off the sheets and swung his legs over the side of the bed. Ak'is raised his head, saw nothing of importance, and went back to sleep. "But my hunches are usually right. If I come across anything else, I'll let you know."

"Same here," Bilagody said. "Arthur?"

"What?"

"Maybe you should rethink handling this alone."

"Who says I'm going to be alone?" This time, Arthur paused. "I have friends everywhere."

"Either way, I'd be very careful." There was seriousness to Jake's tone now. "I wouldn't put it past Thorne to start tracking your cell phone. If he thinks you're close to Kanesewah, he'll want to find you. I saw a report on one of those cable news channels the other night that said the feds have at least a hundred planes wandering the skies every day, flying low and outfitted with high-tech cameras on their bellies, and simulated cell towers inside them that can force your phone to connect to them."

Arthur rattled off his room number and the motel phone number. "Guess I'd better get off, then, before the NSA triangulates my position and launches a missile up my ass."

"Hey!" Jake said, "that isn't funny!"

Arthur tapped the red END prompt on the screen before Jake could finish his thought. Standing up, he crossed the room and felt the cold linoleum bathroom floor on his bare soles. He flicked on the light and removed the plastic wrapping from one of the glasses on the round plastic tray by the mini coffee-maker and ice bucket, and filled it with water. While he drank, he caught himself actually looking forward to the continental breakfast in the morning. The desk clerk manning the long brown front desk with the black polished stoneware top had promised him a delicious array of juices, coffee, cereals, biscuits and gravy, waffles, and other traveler's fare in the breakfast area across from where they were standing. Arthur had decided on biscuits and gravy and a few cups of coffee. He planned to eat at one of the small square tables he had seen by the windows.

Finishing his sterile glass of room-temperature water, he set it on the floating vanity and slapped the light off. If the FBI could turn up anything useful, Jake would make it known in the morning. Arthur went over to the window, grabbed the dangling wands, and parted the curtains. The rain had turned to snow in the last hour of his drive and had only now stopped falling. Everything he could see before him had been covered in a fresh white blanket of frosty stillness. His eyes tracked a plane as it crawled across the empty black sky. Its navigational lights flashed their irregular patterns while its landing lights illuminated the clouds ahead of it like giant flashlight beams searching a smoke-filled room. He was idly wondering where its passengers were going and what they were going to do when they arrived there, when his attention turned to the bare trickle of vehicles moving along the interstate. He paused briefly but decided it wasn't worth the effort wondering where they were going and what they were going to do, so he pulled the curtains back together and shuffled back to the bed.

After climbing in, he pulled the sheets up to his neck and succumbed quickly to sleep's beckoning call, with the sense that he was closer to finding Sharon. Or maybe it was just the hope of the desperate, tugging at his consciousness. Either way, his instincts told him he was getting closer. And if the runners were moving by night in these mountains, they would be having a slow go of it. The bad visibility and slick roads would surely force Kanesewah to slow down and delay him a little. He couldn't take the chance of losing control and ending up in a ditch.

Arthur drifted off, hoping that tomorrow would bring him something more substantial than mere speculation to bolster his hope. Tomorrow would bring with it a … what had Edward once called it? *Diné niyol.* A Navajo wind.

CHAPTER NINETEEN

The jagged peaks of the Teton Range were barely visible above the lodgepole pine forest, their craggy contours muted by the falling snow. It had already begun to cling to the pines and the ground, though not yet to the road they were traveling on. Sharon had turned toward the back seat passenger-side window to make it harder for Leonard to look over his shoulder and ogle her breasts.

As they rolled up Highway 191, Sharon stared out the window, seeing and not seeing the dark expanse of Jackson Lake beyond the trees. She couldn't yet tell whether the inklings of doubt she had planted in Gloria's mind were gathering strength. At this stage, she knew she must use the utmost delicacy, feeding that doubt without appearing too interested, until its relentless nagging at Gloria's subconscious either turned her into an ally or, at the very least, upset the dynamic between her two captors. Then again, if it did the latter, Kanesewah might start viewing both women as unnecessary. When she thought about it, her odds of getting through this alive seemed about as likely as winning the lottery.

If she didn't shift her focus, she would scream. She remembered the morning, just before this nightmare began, when she and Arthur discussed having children, for the first time in what seemed an eternity. That had been the first step. And this time, she wanted to see it through. It was the one thing they were missing, the one thing that could get them back to where they were before. And the thought of creating a life and holding that life and nurturing it, sharing its joys and sorrows, its victories and disappointments, and seeing its potential to become more than they themselves would ever be, was wondrous to contemplate. Tucking that thought into a private corner of her mind where it could keep her warm and calm, she pulled up the blanket and tried to close her eyes.

She had started to doze off when Kanesewah jerked the steering wheel and stomped the brake. Her eyes flew open in time to see the white-tail buck and doe that had darted across the roadway. Gloria woke from her sound sleep as her head slammed the window. She let out a string of expletives in Spanish and then English, which brought a laugh from Leonard. While the two bickered, Sharon tried to locate whatever had tapped her right foot during the evasive maneuver. Reaching with the toe of her shoe beneath Gloria's seat, she felt something solid. She gazed out the window while sliding the right edge of her foot behind the object and slowly pulling it back toward her.

She squirmed in her seat as if trying to get comfortable, and let her eyes sweep across the cell phone that lay on the carpeted floor mat. Covering it with her foot, she prayed that it not come to life with whatever ringtone its murdered owner had chosen. All she had to do now was keep it concealed until she could get a hand on it and slip it into a pocket. If it still had battery power, and if they stopped somewhere that could reel in enough signal to send a text …

* * *

For the next five hours, the cell phone lay concealed beneath her foot. All the while, she kept making mental notes of everything they passed, trying to remember it all. A highway sign would be a godsend, a town's name the holy grail. She remembered the tension of passing through the south entrance of Yellowstone: Kanesewah calmly showing the pass from when they had entered Tetons, the ranger glancing at it and then at the three of them as the snow continued to fall and melt against the warm windshield. Then the gate had gone up and Kanesewah drove through, and Sharon let out the breath she hadn't known she was holding. She recalled skirting the eastern edge of Lewis Lake, heading northwest at the West Thumb of Yellowstone Lake, then seeing nothing but dark wooded wilderness. She remembered seeing a park sign for Old Faithful then crossing more water. Then she remembered breathing in the nauseating sulfur fumes rising from the mud pots and fumaroles that covered the area.

They had driven on for quite a while before crossing Nez Perce Creek, then followed the twists and turns of the Firehole River until it disappeared into the more mountainous darkness.

Then they crossed another river. *The Jefferson—yes, that was it!* And just before the highway split, they had passed some campground. What was it called? She struggled for the name. *Madison—Madison Campground!* Pushing her mind further, she remembered a slight grade coming out of the basin on Highway 89. The blasting heater pulled in more of the pungent sulfur smell. Gloria made a wry remark, and Kanesewah chided her to keep quiet; they would be out of it soon enough.

Sharon moved through her mind, trying to remember the name of the river that now rolled silently by in the snowy darkness to their right … *the Gibbon!* She was pleased with herself for remembering it. *Too many damn rivers in this high country.* From now on, she would try to note only the prominent landmarks that might give Arthur a solid trail to follow. Kanesewah had planned this route well. The road would be open and plowed until it closed for the winter in December. And, unless the snow really dumped, they would be through the north gate without any difficulty, provided that the rangers at that entrance didn't already know of their existence.

As they passed Nymph Lake, Kanesewah suggested to Gloria that someone had named it "Nympho Lake" after her. Her hand sprang up, signaling that he was number one. He laughed. She lit a cigarette and offered it to him. He leaned over, and she slid the filtered end between his lips before lighting another for herself. Both dropped their windows a few inches to circulate the air. Sharon held her breath until the pungent smoke began to escape through the openings, then she pulled the blanket closer—all while keeping her foot on her newly found treasure.

"I have to pee again," Gloria said.

"Jesus Christ, where in hell do you think I should pull over and let this fucking event happen?"

"I don't know," she said, "but you'd better find somewhere before I piss on this seat!"

He muttered, "Woman, you're getting to be a pain in my ass."

Another mile rolled by before Kanesewah spotted a pullout on the left side of the road. Tucked in behind some trees was a stone structure with log trusses holding up a cedar-shake roof. He slid the Yukon into the small parking area beside the structure.

"That's not a bathroom!" Gloria said.

"Look," he told her flatly, "you've gotta piss and so do I. We're a long way from Helena, so just get out and piss!"

"This is bullshit!" she said. "There's got to be something farther up."

"Fucking broads," he growled as he dropped the shift lever into gear and pulled away.

They drove in silence, passing two more pullouts that resembled the one they had left behind. Gloria pointed frantically at an expansive paved parking area. Kanesewah pulled in next to the small unisex facility that all national parks offered now to save on building costs and political backlash, and parked so the Yukon's headlights illuminated the structure. Gloria darted from the truck, ran to the building, and flung open the door.

Sharon decided this might be her only chance. She told Leonard that she had to go, too, and he grudgingly agreed. Gloria emerged from the building into the headlights and walked back to the truck. Sharon knew she would have only an instant. When Kanesewah opened his door and got out and Gloria opened hers to get in, she snatched up the cell phone and slid it beneath the blanket.

"Fuck, it's cold!" Gloria exclaimed as she directed the warming dash vents toward her.

"When I come back, you can take her," Kanesewah said, slamming his door.

Gloria turned to look at Sharon. "Well, I guess everybody's gotta go sometime," she said, grinning at her own double entendre.

Kanesewah was back in barely a minute. Then Gloria led Sharon to the small building. Sharon had managed to slip the cell phone into a front pocket of her pants before stepping into the freezing mountain cold with the blanket wrapped around her. They walked to the shelter.

"I thought you said he cares about you," Sharon said.

"Shut up," Gloria snapped. "You don't know shit. I'm tired of uppity bitches like you thinkin' their shit don't stink and talkin' about my life like they know anything about it."

"Okay, I'm sorry," Sharon said. "I just think he's using you. Or haven't you ever given any thought to what he'll do when he doesn't need you anymore?"

"I said, shut the fuck up!" Gloria pulled the revolver from her coat pocket and pressed the muzzle against Sharon's back. "Get it?"

Sharon nodded. "If you don't mind, I'd like some privacy this time."

Gloria sighed. "Christ. You think I'm gonna watch you piss?" She glanced toward the SUV, squinting against the bluish glare of the headlights. "Whatever, bitch. Just get it done. And don't fuck around. I'm freezing my *coño* off."

Sharon stepped into the small room and closed the door behind her, locking it while banging the seat to mask the sound. Goose bumps covered her bare legs as she slipped her slacks and panties down to her knees and steeled herself. After the initial shock of contact with the cold seat, she pulled the phone from her pants pocket. She flipped the antique open with her thumb, and the small screen lit up. No signal bars meant no hope of getting a message out. But the battery was at full charge, and she had to try. Even if the signal found no way out now, it would keep trying until it hit that magic spot in the cellular galaxy where it would be allowed to slip through the digital veil and get to Arthur.

She made the expected noises for Gloria while discovering that the phone wasn't password protected. Two seconds later, she had located the text function. She was relieved that the owner had disabled the key click function, perhaps after hearing news reports of robberies in which store clerks had been killed when the key clicks gave them away.

As Sharon emptied her bladder, she thumbed the small keys as fast as she could.

```
may b only chance to contact
somewhere north of Yellowstone
heading for great falls
then canada
brown yukon mn plt
find me I luv u
S
```

Gloria pounded on the door. "Hurry up, bitch! My fuckin' lips are freezing together! Both sets!"

She went to settings and changed the ringtone to "none," closed the phone, and stuck it back in her pocket. She stood and collected herself, then opened the door.

"'Bout fucking time," Gloria said, looking into the small room. She sniffed, then said with a surprised grin, "I guess your shit really doesn't stink."

CHAPTER TWENTY

Morning hit hard as the clock radio on the nightstand exploded with a forgotten eighties hair-band hit. Arthur woke facedown in his hotel pillows and reached out in a blind effort to silence the onslaught of wailing guitars and screaming lyrics, but all his fumbling did was knock his cell phone to the floor. The hair band screamed on. He opened one eye long enough to find the radio's sweet spot and send the band back to rock-and-roll oblivion, then flopped back down in the short stack of pillows.

But it was no good—he couldn't get back to sleep. Now that he was awake, his mind raced with possible scenarios out of his control. He turned his head to the left and met with Ak'is' patient stare. The screaming band had roused him, too. Arthur scratched the wolf-dog's head and rolled over onto his back, extending both legs in a stretch that quickly took over his whole body. He rolled his head over again. Ak'is' patience was surpassed only by his persistence. And right now that meant only one thing—he wasn't about to pay for carpet cleaning.

"Sometimes you're a pain," he said as he rolled out of bed.

Retrieving his cell phone from the floor, he pitched it onto the bed and put on yesterday's clothes. Then he pocketed his room card, dropped the phone into his shirt pocket, and walked out the door, leaving the DO NOT DISTURB tag hanging on the knob. Ak'is led the way down the absurdly decorated hallway toward the lobby. Arthur had never thought of using a leash on him and wasn't about to start now. The animal was always free to do as he pleased.

Passing the front desk, they drew curious stares from the clerk and the free-breakfast crowd. Arthur could hear the faint whispers circling among the handful of people sipping and noshing in the breakfast area and ignored them. Ak'is' nostrils flared at the scents of bacon and sausage, and Arthur could swear that he saw him lick his chops on their way out. They wandered around just past the parking lot until the animal found a suitable spot where he could make a deposit. Then it was back to the room.

After shedding his clothes and jumping in the shower, Arthur was out in ten minutes and pulling on fresh underwear, jeans, socks, and a long-sleeved khaki shirt from his duffel. The shirt was only slightly wrinkled from its military roll, and he didn't care whether anyone noticed. Out of habit, he picked up his cell phone and held his thumb over the button to unlock it. Who said he wasn't with the times?

The phone lit up, displaying all its applications, most of which Arthur never used and kept threatening to delete someday. The blue square holding the little white envelope appeared with a small "2" in the upper right corner. He tapped it, and a half a moment later he saw the *Find Russian Brides* and the *Drastic Change to your Credit Score* emails. He deleted them both and tossed the phone back onto the bed. He had made it as far as the bathroom before the phone on the nightstand rang. He returned to the bed, sat down, and picked up the receiver. It was Jake Bilagody. Some new information had come to light. Thorne had been right. Hidden somewhere in a forgotten file regarding Kanesewah's violent history was a name.

"A Gloria Sanchez," Bilagody was telling him. "Seems that when they conducted several interviews with his people on the San Carlos rez, they spoke to a young woman named Nashota Kah-Zhe. She had dated Kanesewah before Sanchez showed up. Anyway, this woman said our boy has an angry side. Real mean. 'Sadistic' was the word she used."

"No kidding," Arthur said. "He beat her?"

"That's why she left him. Gave her a black eye more than once and broke her left arm *twice*. She said this Sanchez came into the picture about a month after she ran out on him."

"They find Sanchez yet?"

"FBI went to her apartment in Globe. Looks like she packed quick and left quicker. Hasn't been at her job in days, and her car is missing. A brown '87 Buick Regal."

Jake gave Arthur the license number, and he typed it into the "Notes" app on his cell phone. Some apps did come in handy, it seemed.

"Thorne's got every cop in the Mountain time zone looking for that car. He's pulled his troops from downstate and has them heading up your way. He's also trying to commandeer a helicopter or two. Wants to throw a wide net, he said."

"Sure," Arthur said.

"What's your next move?"

"Keep following my gut and continue north. At least now I have something solid to look for. Any way you can get me a picture of Sanchez?"

"I'll email it to you," Jake said. "If you can't open the attachment, I'll text it."

"Listen to you, sounding all tech-savvy," Arthur said. "Makes me think you know what you're doing."

"Screw you. My granddaughter showed me how to do some things. Kid knows more about this stuff than I ever will."

"It's their world, my friend. We just live in it. I'll be looking for the picture. Right now my continental breakfast is calling."

The breakfast area was an L-shaped affair with contractor-grade cabinetry and the usual lithographed mountain scenes adorning the papered walls. The well-worn cream-colored ceramic tile floor was set with small square tables and cushioned wooden chairs. He opened one of the stainless warmers to find the sausage gravy, then took three biscuits from the clear plastic beehive to its right and ladled on the gravy. Stepping around to the small row of coffeepots, he stuck his cup under the spout and pulled the triangular lever of the one marked "Mountain Blend." He watched the cup fill to within half an inch of the lip before he let the lever up, then dumped in three creams from an ice-filled bucket and grabbed a stir stick. He picked his silverware from the three round containers set at an angle on the counter and put them in the front pocket of his jeans. Then he picked up his plate of biscuits and gravy and wandered to a small square table by a window and sat.

Arthur swished the little flat stick and turned the coffee into the proper shade of tan before cutting a wedge of gravy-covered biscuit. He was enjoying the taste when his cell phone buzzed and vibrated in his shirt pocket. Laying down his fork, he pulled the phone out and put his thumb against it. A number 1 showed up in a red circle by the little white envelope outlined in blue. He tapped it. The application opened, and there was Jake's email titled "Sanchez pic."

The familiar clockwise spinning circle told him the photo was loading. When it popped up, he saw a pretty but rough Latina face framed by shoulder-length black hair. Gloria Sanchez now had an image to go with the name. He saved the photo and put the phone away, then spent the next fifteen minutes finishing his breakfast and pondering the day ahead.

Arthur's phone buzzed in his pocket again. He wondered what new information Jake could be sending him now, then was puzzled by the 218 area code. And he didn't recognize the phone number displayed in the green bar alerting him to the text. He tapped his fingertip against the screen and opened the message.

CHAPTER TWENTY-ONE

```
may b only chance to contact
somewhere north of Yellowstone
heading for great falls
then canada
brown yukon mn plt
find me I luv u
S
```

Arthur's breath trembled as the words *find me* repeated over and over in his mind. Suddenly self-conscious, he glanced around the breakfast area. Had anyone heard him? If so, they paid him no mind. Most were caught up in conversations that he tuned out and turned to white noise. Others stared at the flat-panel TV mounted on the wall by the faux-pillared entrance, watching the breaking report on the latest car bombing in Kabul.

That's my girl, he thought. She had done it. He had hoped she would find a way of contacting him, and he knew that she had taken a grave risk doing it. Kanesewah would make her pay for it, and he didn't want to think of how. Would he beat her for her betrayal? Kill her? Not if he still thought she could be used as a bargaining chip. Arthur quickly pulled himself back into the reality that surrounded him, remembering what Jake Bilagody had said about Special Agent Thorne and cell phones. He dialed the commuting chief's number on the walk back to his motel room.

Jake Bilagody picked up as Arthur pulled the key card from its slot in the door lock and went inside. Ak'is wagged his bushy tail in anticipation. Seeing and smelling nothing, the wolf-dog stepped away from him and lay down on the floor, doing the canine version of a pout. Arthur told Bilagody about the text.

"Then that rings true with the information we got just after I sent you the picture," Jake said. "A couple in their seventies from Minnesota vacationing in Jackson Hole had their Yukon stolen last night. Sanchez's Buick was found next to the spot where the SUV had been parked in the lot. They found the old man's body in a dumpster at the end of the motel. He'd been stabbed to death." Jake paused. "Hell of a way to die."

"Did anyone see anything?" Arthur asked. "Anyone see Sharon?"

"There was a guy that walked to the motel office earlier last evening," he said. "He claims to have seen the car parked in a different spot in the lot. Thought there may have been three people in it—two in the front seat and one in the back—but it was too dark to make out any faces."

"Damn it, I'm *this* close, Jake!" Arthur said. "They were only four hours or so ahead of me last night." He paused to let that soak in. "I shouldn't have stopped, tired or not."

"You can't think like that," Jake said. "What good would you be to Sharon cracked up at the bottom of a ravine somewhere because you fell asleep? Besides, Thorne and his bunch are already there. They converged on Jackson Hole like Sitting Bull coming down on Custer's Seventh Cavalry." Jake chuckled. "Kanesewah's probably already gone to ground somewhere in Montana by now."

Arthur thought about that for a moment. "You think you could run a check on where the number Sharon texted from pinged off a tower last?"

"Probably," Jake replied. "I know a guy I can call."

"You know a guy?" Arthur said.

"What makes you think I can't know a guy? I'm a sworn officer of the law with over twenty years' experience and an extensive list of guys I know."

"I'm gonna toss my stuff together and head toward Helena. Call me when you know something."

It hadn't taken long—less than twenty minutes, in fact. Arthur was throwing his gear in the back of the Bronco when his cell phone vibrated again. It was Jake. The guy he knew had run the number and located the cell tower where Sharon's phone last pinged. The explanation was too full of computer jargon to be of any use, but there were six towers in Livingston, Montana. The first one was owned by Cold Creek Cellular. He could pinpoint it with latitude and longitude if Arthur wanted him to, but that wasn't necessary. The next ping came from a tower at Meyers Flat. That was on Route 89 on the way up to Great Falls.

"If he's heading up that way," Jake said, "it means he's still staying off the Interstates and sticking to the less-traveled routes. And this traveling by night and keeping contact to a minimum seems to be working for him." Jake paused. "The old guy's Yukon is the third vehicle he's stolen since this all began. And it's a four-wheel-drive, too. What does that tell you?"

"It tells me Kanesewah will be trying to get to Canada the rough-and-tumble way," Arthur replied. "But I don't think he'll have any easy way to get through the Montana Rockies in a Yukon." Now Arthur paused, thinking. "He'll have to go off road and get as deep as he can get with the truck before dumping it and trying to hump it the rest of the way on foot." Arthur shook his head. "He must have started planning this after he realized he screwed up with the Braun girl. He isn't just running. He has a schedule, and he has his route already planned out. If they get caught in a big snow up there, they'll freeze to death. But then, Kanesewah probably thought about that, too."

Jake said, "Sharon is going to pass three more towers before they get into the Lewis and Clark National Forest. That's where they'll probably go dark until they come out the northern side of the forest and start heading toward Great Falls. There's almost three thousand square miles of pristine wilderness, and one road right through the middle of it. My guy says after that, there are over twenty cell towers surrounding Great Falls. I told him to keep me posted, and if it pinged off any of them, I wanted to know about it. She might try to contact you again if she gets the chance." Jake paused, as if weighing something. "I guess you already thought about texting her back? Letting her know you got it?"

"I was born at night," Arthur replied, "but it wasn't last night. If that phone she's got makes any kind of sound, she's screwed."

Arthur thanked the chief, disconnected the call, and put the phone back into his pocket. Helena was almost an eight-hour drive on a good day with no weather to contend with. And adding another hour to get to Great Falls meant he would have to drive nonstop to catch up. But it was now daylight, and Kanesewah would be in hiding. That would give him the time he needed. He was also thinking that the trip could be made even longer if the snow that seemed to be hanging in the graying skies decided to cut loose. *Damn this early fall mountain weather, anyway.* He longed for the milder conditions of his own high desert.

Arthur pulled open the passenger door, and Ak'is jumped in. When he slammed the door shut, it rang with that same hollow metal sound that old truck doors made when they passed the thirty-year mark. Had it been that way for the past fifteen years and he simply hadn't noticed until now? He paused as a hint of realization settled in. A lot of things had been catching up to him since Sharon was taken from him. As he circled around and climbed in, he wondered how he had become so oblivious to the details of life. He started the engine and shut the door—another hollow metal clang.

Time was going to become a scarce commodity, and he could not waste a second of it. An errant thought came out of nowhere, and he pulled his phone out, opened his contacts list, and tapped a name, then a number. When the call finally went through, he took a deep breath and hoped the familiar voice would answer on the other end.

The last time he had seen Abraham Fasthorse was before they left the Shadow Wolves. The day the Wolf pack had gone hunting for a rip crew thought to be part of the Sinaloa Cartel.

They had tracked the team of two armed guards and ten smugglers carrying drug-filled burlap backpacks to the steep ravine known as the Crow's Nest, on the Tohono Odum rez. It was a well-known place where smugglers liked to hole up during the day before traveling at night. The human mules had worn booties made from carpet scraps, lashed to their feet so they wouldn't leave behind any prints. But that never fooled the Wolves. And neither did the smugglers' trick of walking with small herds of wandering cattle when they had to cut across some of the smaller ranches, to throw off the trackers.

The pack had cut sign for six hours in the blazing desert heat and had just finished fanning out into a wide line before heading down into the ravine, when Arthur caught the scent of marijuana on the breeze. Sometimes, in the heat of the day, they would pick up the strong smell of pot moistened by the sweating backs of the men carrying it. Just then automatic gunfire from two AK-47s echoed in the dusk. The pack instantly returned fire with their M4s. The firefight lasted ten minutes. And when the automatic fire had stopped, the smugglers' armed guards lay dead, along with six of the poor souls who had been forced to pack the marijuana. Abraham Fasthorse was on the ground, holding his legs and writhing in the sand in a creosote thicket. Bullets from an AK had ripped into his thighs, narrowly missing both femoral arteries but causing major damage all the same. Arthur quickly pulled off his belt and fashioned a tourniquet around one leg. He repeated the task with his partner's belt while yelling, "Officer down!"

Someone radioed for Air Unit Omaha, the helicopter aiding them in the search from the CBP's Air and Marine Operations, to come and get his friend to the nearest hospital as fast as it could. And it had done just that. Now the ringing in his ear stopped, replaced by the voice of Abraham Fasthorse. Arthur smiled.

"*Oki Ni-kso-ko-wa*," Arthur said. His command of the Blackfoot language was feeble, at best and "Hello, greetings, my kinsman" was all he could remember of what Fasthorse had taught him.

"Not half bad for a desert dweller," Fasthorse said. "I almost thought you were a real Blackfoot."

"It's all I could remember, my friend." Arthur got right to the point. "I need your help."

"I have seen the news," Fasthorse told him. "How are you holding up and what do you need from me?"

"I'm fine. Listen, back in the day, you told me of the network of brothers up in the Nation. I'm on my way to you, leaving Rock Springs, Wyoming, as we speak. I need you to get the word out to the brothers to look for a brownish GMC Yukon with Minnesota plates. Should be coming out of the Lewis and Clark National Forest tonight and heading toward Great Falls."

"I will circulate the word to keep an eye out for this Chiricahua man and his woman. If he is in our country, we will find him."

"They stay hidden during the day and travel by night," Arthur told him, "so I should be able to get to Great Falls by the time they do, if not before. They'll be going to ground now, so I'll try to get there by sundown. That's when they'll be on the move again."

"Like the cockroach," Fasthorse said. "They only come out in darkness." He paused. "You are my brother, Nakai, and it would be my honor to help you. When you get here, we will talk. Maybe I will have some news."

"It'll be just like the Wolves, brother," Arthur said.

"Once a tracker, always a tracker," Fasthorse said. "He will not escape us."

"I'm counting on it," Arthur said and put the truck in drive.

CHAPTER TWENTY-TWO

"What the fuck you waiting for?" Gloria barked. "Get to it! You got your fucking sink and a chance for a bath, so hurry the fuck up and get moving. I've got what you got, so get to washing it up."

She held the .38 pointed in the general direction, with an attitude more of laziness than of urgency. She stood with her back against the grungy bathroom door, looking bored. Her mouth worked a piece of gum as if it were a tough steak. The look on her face told Sharon she wasn't facing the task with any real exuberance.

Sharon began to undress under the harsh, buzzing fluorescent tubes in the cramped gas station bathroom. The station wasn't one of those big, brightly lit monstrosities with the oversize awning and twenty gas pumps with TVs on them. It was just a mom-and-pop off-brand on the outskirts of Great Falls, Montana, which had been forced to add a handicapped stall, squashing the original stall to the point where you had to have scoliosis just to fit inside. The kind, Sharon thought, that made you want to get a tetanus shot just for walking through the creaking metal door.

Gloria waved the pistol. "Faster, bitch. We ain't got all night."

Sharon shrugged off her blazer and held it out to her captor.

"Just drop it on the floor. I'll pick it up when you're done." Then she added with a smirk, "Miss TV had to have a bath, said she was feeling unclean. His head must be getting as soft as his *pito.*"

With a cringe, Sharon dropped the blazer on the grimy floor. Her blouse went next, and she made sure it landed on top of the blazer. Then she kicked off her shoes and unfastened the narrow belt. When she unhooked the slacks, she felt the weight of the cell phone in her pants pocket and froze. Moving slowly, mind whirling, she tried to figure a way to keep it hidden.

There had been no time to prepare. No time to slip it into a hiding place in the SUV. No time when she wasn't constantly watched. They had left the concealment of the woods and driven the rest of the way into town as night fell over the mountains. They had managed to find their way to this ratty gas station and the even rattier bathroom and pushed her into it. Now Gloria Sanchez was waving the pistol at the filthy tile floor.

Gripping the waistband and belt tightly but with feigned nonchalance, she slid her slacks to the floor and stepped out of them. Now, down to her pink Cosabella bra and panties, she stood shivering, humiliated and scared. She tried crossing her arms to control the shivering, but it didn't help. She watched Gloria squat down by the duffel bag she had brought in and pull out a black trash bag.

She motioned with her chin toward Sharon's underwear. "Bet your husband got you those, huh?"

Sharon didn't answer. Gloria kept her eyes trained on her while pawing through the duffel. She stood and tossed Sharon a small dry rag.

"Use the soap in the dispenser and make it quick."

The glaring fluorescent lights flickered and buzzed as Sharon turned on the scratched and nicked faucet and held the rag under the icy water. When the water turned lukewarm, she squirted a green blob of soap onto the rag and worked it into a lather. She washed her hands and arms, darting furtive sideways glances between Gloria and the rumpled pile of clothes on the floor. If Sanchez were to pick them up to shove them into the garbage bag, she would feel the unexplained weight. And she would take the phone to Kanesewah.

She scrubbed under her arms and between her breasts, pulling the lace bra away from her skin to keep it from getting soaked. Then, rinsing the rag in the now tepid water, she added more soap, rubbed it to a healthy lather again, and began washing her face. She had to think of something and think fast. It was time to water the seeds of doubt she had already planted.

"Has he ever told you he loves you?" Sharon said, slipping the rag around two fingers and rubbing in a circular motion on her cheeks, looking in the mirror at Gloria. "I bet he's never even told you, right?"

Gloria shook her head. "What the fuck are you talking about? Don't try to pull none of that psychological bullshit on me. We're not college roomies talking about boyfriends, so don't make out like you care about my life, because I really don't give a shit about yours." Then she muttered under her breath, "Don't even know why he brought you, anyway … Should have just killed you."

Sharon self-consciously pushed the matching lace panties down and washed her thighs, crotch, buttocks.

"I haven't heard him say 'I love you' once," Sharon said. "How can you even be sure he's going to go through with whatever it is he's promised you at the end of all this?"

"I told you once to shut the fuck up, and I meant it, bitch." Gloria stepped forward, toward the pile of dirty clothes on the floor, the .38 trained on Sharon's midsection. "You don't know shit."

Sharon doused the rag in the sink and rinsed the soap off her, then turned off the water and folded the rag and laid it over the edge of the sink. She had been surprised by Gloria's metamorphosis during this whole ordeal, from timid submissive to willing accomplice. She hadn't figured on that.

"Doesn't it bother you," she asked, pulling up her panties, "that he's killed all those other women? And the sixteen-year-old girl he just tortured and killed and raped the other day?" She stood looking directly at Gloria, smelling of antibacterial soap and not shivering anymore. "He's killed two people just while I've been a part of this, and one of them was my friend—a good man with a family. How could you even love someone like that? Let alone trust him?" She stepped toward the pile of clothes on the floor, starting to shiver again now that the warmth of the water was gone. "How do you think he got the SUV? He murdered that man for it back there. I saw him do it. You were turned around looking at me, or you would have seen it, too. It was horrible."

"Shut the fuck up, I said!"

Sharon stepped closer. "You'd better wake up and realize

what kind of man you're with. What makes you think he won't do the same to you?"

"I said, shut the fuck up!" The gun trembled in Gloria's hand. She kicked the duffel across the floor, and it slid to a stop at Sharon's feet. "Dig out some clothes and put them on and just shut the fuck up already! I'm tired of your mouth!"

"Okay," Sharon said calmly. "Okay."

Squatting down, she reached inside the bag with both hands. She fished around and pulled out a pair of jeans and a red-and-black flannel shirt and stood back up. She draped the shirt over the scratched and graffitied wall of the toilet stall and got into the jeans. They fit a little loose, but the shirt helped snug them up when she put it on and tucked it in. She was buttoning it up when Gloria said, "Put your shoes back on and don't fucking talk to me. I'm done listening to your bullshit."

Gloria squatted down and picked up the black trash bag, held one side between her teeth while she worked her fingers into the plastic to open it, pulled it apart, and shook it. She snatched the clothes off the floor and shoved the blouse and jacket into the bag, then paused with the pants still in her hand. She looked up at Sharon and stood up, dropped the trash bag on the floor, and held the pants with her gun hand while searching the pockets with the other. Her hand emerged with the phone..

"You fucking bitch," she said. "How long have you had this?"

Sharon said nothing.

"Oh, you're dead now, lady," she said. "You are so fucking dead."

She picked up the trash bag, stuffed the pants into it, and put the cell phone in the front pocket of her jeans. "Move!" she barked, waving the gun. "NOW!"

Sharon stepped toward the bathroom door.

"Open it. And say goodbye, bitch. I can't wait to show him your little fucking toy."

Sharon opened the door, and they walked out into the icy Montana night. Tiny flakes of snow had fallen while the two were in the bathroom, and everything wore a thin veil of white. Sharon breathed in the smell of gas and hoped it would not be the last thing she ever smelled.

* * *

In the warmth of the Yukon, Kanesewah noticed the .38 trained on Sharon.

"What's with the gun?" he said. "She grab your ass or something?"

Grinning, Gloria pulled the cell phone out of her pocket and rocked it tauntingly. "I found this in her pants," she said, handing it to him. "She won't tell me where she got it or how long she's had it. But you can bet your ass she's used it."

A slow anger began to build in Kanesewah's face, and he glared at Sharon in the back seat. Finally, he brought his right forearm down hard, slamming it onto the leather console between the bucket seats.

"What did I tell you I'd do if I caught you trying to contact anyone?" he said through gritted teeth.

Sharon sat quietly, her mind working on not giving him an answer. She felt the back of his hand smash against her face and tasted the blood from her nose and lips. The blow had knocked her back against the seat, which bounced her down to the floor of the second-row seats. She had started to push herself up when the same big hand grabbed her hair and jerked her head backward. In that fleeting window, she noticed Gloria smiling.

Kanesewah tossed the phone to her and held Sharon's head with both hands. One held a fistful of black hair while the other gripped her jaw, its thumb and fingers squeezing her face into a distorted and bloody caricature of herself.

"When we get to a place where we're alone, I am going to skin you like a deer." He paused, his breathing heavy, her warm blood spilling across his fingers. "And you'll be alive when I start." A disturbed grin appeared on his face. "I can't say how you'll be when I finish, but I know that long before that, you will be praying for death to come."

He flung her backward, slamming her left temple into the armrest of her seat, and she slid to the floor again. Struggling against the pain, she climbed back into her seat, unbuttoned the right sleeve of her flannel shirt, and began wiping the blood from her face. Her breath was fast and shallow. It felt as though he had broken her nose, because it had already begun to swell and she was having trouble drawing air through it. Kanesewah took back the cell phone from Gloria, flipped it open, and thumbed some buttons. Apparently finding nothing of interest, he pushed more buttons. He glanced at Gloria, then stared at Sharon. "Who did you text?"

She didn't answer.

The hand struck again, bouncing her head off the leather headrest. More blood came, and her neck hurt. She covered her face with her hands as the pain coursed through her. She saw the hand cock back for a third time, and put her hand out to fend it off.

"My husband!" she yelled through fingers now glistening with blood. "I sent a message to my husband!"

Kanesewah twisted around in the driver's seat to face her. "You wasted your life to text your husband?" He laughed as he read the message. "Who is he?"

Sharon stared at him as blood began to mix with the red of her flannel shirt. "He's the man who is going to hunt you down and kill you."

The corner of Kanesewah's mouth twitched as he looked at Gloria. She looked at him, then at Sharon. "You have a lot of faith in this husband of yours," he said.

"Oh, I do," Sharon replied, noticing a thought behind his eyes. "Do you fear him? You should."

Kanesewah scoffed. "Don't read into my mind something that isn't there. I fear no one."

"I know that look when I see it," Sharon said, patting her face gently with her other shirtsleeve, trying to soak up the darkening blood. "You should be afraid, because when he finds you, he's going to kill you. And if you kill me, he's going to do it very slowly. And knowing him, he's probably already here."

Kanesewah scoffed again, "What do you mean 'here'?"

Sharon looked at him. "We travel by night. He travels by day *and* night. You figure it out."

Kanesewah looked at the number she had texted and dialed it.

He was looking at Gloria's worried expression when someone answered. He put the call on speaker.

"*Abini Sin*," Arthur said. "Where are you?

"She's in the backseat, bleeding," Kanesewah replied.

A second ticked by, then another. "Let me talk to her."

Kanesewah looked at Sharon. "I don't think that will be possible right now. Like I said, she's busy trying to stop bleeding."

"If any harm comes to my wife, you're going to know what hell feels like."

Kanesewah looked at his woman and grinned. "Oh, I've already harmed her, Husband. The question is, am I going to kill her? And the answer to that will depend on you."

Sharon had managed to slow the blood, with the aid of some fast-food napkins from the pouch behind the passenger seat, which she used to plug her nostrils. She could feel the bruising begin, and the swelling of her lip and the tissue around her nose. When the paper-napkin plugs couldn't hold any more blood, she replaced them with fresh ones, and soon the floor in front of her was dotted with red-and-white cones of wadded paper.

Arthur's voice turned cold. "You need to know that I am capable of terrible things when someone threatens the people I love."

"And you should know," Kanesewah replied, "that I am capable of much more terrifying things than you could ever imagine."

Arthur's jaw muscles tensed as his hand gripped the phone tighter. "I am going to track you down and separate every limb from your body."

Kanesewah smiled. "You think I'm afraid of you, Husband?" He let his question hang in the air. "I am not afraid of you."

"Then that would be your second mistake."

CHAPTER TWENTY-THREE

Arthur's ears strained against the dead silence before he finally pulled the phone from his ear and stared at the words CALL ENDED.

He opened his recent-calls list and tapped Fasthorse's number. The phone rang, and Fasthorse picked up. "Put the Brotherhood on alert," Arthur told him. "They're somewhere in Great Falls. The bastard just had the balls to call me."

"Kanesewah?" Fasthorse said. "I will put the word out in urgency."

"He found the phone Sharon used to contact me, and he's already hurt her." Arthur felt his jaw muscles tighten. "When we find him, I want him."

Fasthorse paused a moment, considering the statement. "Be careful, my friend. Emotions are like fire," he said. "Man fools himself into thinking that he controls fire, but in reality, it is the fire that controls man. And emotions, like fire, are often wild and free beings that live and breathe on their own.

If you are not careful, the fire will consume you."

"I'll try to remember that before I kill him," Arthur said.

Fasthorse breathed a disheartened sigh. "Do you know how to get to my place?"

"Not really."

Fasthorse rattled off directions. "It should take you about forty minutes to get here. I have already begun to gather what we will need."

"Good," Arthur said. "See you in forty."

* * *

Three Suns Outfitters sat at the end of a long gravel road that branched off just before Highway 17 curved north toward Canada on the Blackfoot Reservation. Behind it, the snowcapped mountains of the Lewis Range stood purple in the waning light. Arthur remembered Fasthorse telling him of this land during a Shadow Wolves stakeout. In a rare feat of geological legerdemain, a vast slab of billion-year-old Precambrian rock three miles thick was pushed up and over Cretaceous strata less than a fifth its age, eventually creating the landscape he now drove through. A light snow was falling, bringing with it the prickly chill of winter. If it came down heavily, Arthur reflected, they would surely need the Brotherhood to spot Kanesewah quickly so they could put an end to all this.

Arthur approached the main house, with its weathered elk and bighorn skulls mounted beneath the wide front porch's sloping roof—put there, no doubt, to spark the paying guests' imaginations and get them salivating over the coming hunt.

The two-story log main house probably comprised an office and outfitter shop on the lower level, with Fasthorse's living quarters and maybe some guest suites above. Several small log cabins around the property, which had been filled with hunters, fisherman, and trail riders during the busy season, had already been mothballed until May, when the whole cycle would start over again.

Arthur parked the Bronco on the gravel in front of the main house and turned off the engine. Abraham Fasthorse was already standing at the edge of the porch, above the rough-sawn log steps.

He looked just as Arthur had remembered: tall and lean and muscular. In fact, about the only thing different he could see was that his pitch-black hair had now grown beyond his shoulders. He wore jeans and a dark-brown Carhartt Santa Fe jacket and was massaging his thighs—a lingering reminder of the gun battle at the Crow's Nest. Perhaps, like Arthur, he felt the old wounds more as the colder air approached. Or maybe it was just that the pain stored in a man's body accrued with age.

"*Oki*," Fasthorse said.

"*Yá'át'ééh*," Arthur replied as Ak'is bounded out of the truck after him. They climbed the log steps to the porch. "It's good to see you, my friend."

Fasthorse embraced him. "And who is this?" He nodded at the wolf-dog.

Arthur introduced them and asked Ak'is to stay on the porch. The animal walked over, sniffed a stretched-out piece of carpeting in front of two well-used rocking chairs, and lay down, looking like a furry black-and-gray sphinx.

Fasthorse grinned. "I would think that a man of your stature in the world would have the wherewithal to drive something a little more up-to-date."

Arthur looked at his trusty steed. "I only drive what I know I can still fix. Besides, me and this old truck go way back. Getting rid of it now would be like saying goodbye to a vital organ."

Fasthorse laughed. "Come inside. My wife has food ready. You must be hungry."

The inside of the main house was a warm contrast to the deepening cold outside. The business office was sequestered in a room off to the right, and in front of them, two couches and two chairs, all of mission design, formed a U beneath the elk-antler chandelier before a big stone fireplace. To their left stood tables and chairs, where guests could play cards and have a drink while swapping yarns about the day's hunt.

The outfitting shop filled the rest of the expansive downstairs. It was packed with now mostly-empty clothing racks that had carried the usual hunting and fishing attire, along with some Western and possibly even some traditional Blackfoot clothing. Several fly rods and creels hung on one wall, and the rustic glass-and-oak display case still held fifty different wet and dry flies and a dozen kinds of fishing and hunting knives. A stand-alone three-tiered table had the expected Native American trinkets and souvenirs of a visit in the Blackfoot Nation, which the guests eagerly purchased as mementos of their time roughing it.

Arthur's eyes went to the many calibers and loads of boxed ammunition stacked neatly on the shelves behind the display cases. "You seem to have done well for yourself," he said as Fasthorse took his jacket and slung it on a peg.

Fasthorse smiled. "It keeps a roof over my head and food on my table. When I came back here to live after that mess at the Crow's Nest, I saw again the poverty I had left behind, and decided to create something that would help my people." They sat down at one of the tables. "When I got back to the rez, it was suffering from a tribal police force banking some serious overtime and giving the people very little to show for it. The poverty level was around sixty-seven percent, so I got some people together, and we built this place." Fasthorse looked around the big, open room. "We bought this house, renovated it into what you see now, and built those cabins you saw as you drove in. I employ a staff of twenty-five during the season."

"And a staff of one the rest of the time," said a female voice behind them.

Arthur turned in his chair to see a slender middle-aged woman who had emerged from what must be the kitchen, carrying a big oval tray. The food smelled good. Really good, Arthur realized. A lot better than the biscuits and gravy that had worn off two hundred miles ago. Her long black hair was pulled back in a ponytail that swayed across the back of her red blouse as she walked and stopped just above the long khaki skirt with a turquoise concha belt.

"Annie, meet the infamous Arthur Nakai. Arthur, meet the best thing that has ever happened to me."

She smiled and set the tray on the table between them, expressing to Arthur her knowledge of the sadness that had brought him to their home for the first time, and the expectation that she would soon meet Sharon as well. She smiled and said, "I'll leave you two alone to talk," then kissed her husband goodnight and vanished up the stairs next to the fireplace. Arthur heard a door close somewhere, and there was silence again.

He turned his attention to the tray of food and took care not to drool on the fried chicken and bowls of mashed potatoes, corn, baked beans, and creamy brown gravy.

"Looks good," he said.

"Let's find out," Fasthorse replied.

It was as good as it looked and smelled. They ate in silence.

After they had thrown a sizable dent in the feast, Arthur said, "Been a while since we last chased down some of those *evildoers* Bush Forty-Three always talked about."

Fasthorse put down the chicken leg and gave a fond smile. "No shit. But we had some good times in the Wolves, didn't we? Damn shame that the jackasses up the food chain wouldn't let us catch them after we tracked them down."

"I don't know about you," Arthur said, "but what always bothered me were all those times the Mexican troops crossed over back then. *Two hundred and eighteen* incursions onto US soil, and you never heard anything about it on the news. Not a word."

"That is because the news media are the pawns of the false world, brother," Fasthorse explained. "They only tell the people what they want them to hear. If everyone really knew all that was going on in this country, they would shit their pants." He sipped his coffee. "You think they ever heard of the Mexican paramilitaries that crossed over in January of oh-seven and ran into the National Guard at their surveillance posts? Hell no. And those dudes were packing automatic weapons." He shook his head in disgust. "What really pissed me off was that the Guard had them cold and the AIC ordered them to pull back and not engage."

Arthur pushed away his empty plate and grinned. "Speaking of Assholes in Charge, there's an FBI stiff heading up this case who thinks he knows what to do and doesn't want me getting involved. Well fuck 'im. This time, the Shadow Wolves aren't answering to some suit. This bastard, we get to catch."

"I meant what I said to you earlier, old friend." Fasthorse always had a way of bringing the conversation back to point. "Do not let your rage blind you, or the fire will consume you."

Arthur looked over the rim of his coffee mug. "Is that what you would do if it were Annie?"

"Every man needs to have something he will fight for," Fasthorse said. "Or someone. But we are not talking about me. And I can say this to you because I can be objective. I am looking at this from the outside, and I see the rage building within you. And I am afraid it will get you killed." Fasthorse put his mug down on the table. "And how would I explain that to your wife once I've rescued her?" He grinned. "For that matter, how would I explain it to *mine*?"

"He's already hurt her," Arthur reiterated. "He said she was already bleeding. I spent my entire time driving up here with all kinds of scenarios floating around in my head." He stopped talking, took a deep breath, and blew it out. "I just keep thinking about her being scared. And here I am, so close to this bastard, and I can't even do anything to stop him."

"And you do not think he knows that?" Fasthorse said. "He knows all he has to do is threaten to do something to her so you'll back off and buy him some more time. Look at how you are acting right now." Leaning forward, he rested his forearms on the table, curled the fingers of his right hand, and tapped the wood with his middle finger. "You cannot allow yourself to lose focus. You will not be of any use to her if your head is not clear. And you will need a clear head if we are to take her away from this man."

Arthur considered that statement and even allowed himself to acknowledge its wisdom, to a point. He could not let his emotions rule his thoughts and jeopardize Sharon's safety. In an earlier time, in another part of the world, this would have been a mission. And that mission would have needed him to be razor sharp and 100 percent focused. Lives would have depended on it. This was no different.

"You're right," he conceded finally. "I just hate this waiting around for someone to spot him so we can get moving."

Fasthorse gave an understanding nod. "Do not worry, my friend. If he is out there, the Brotherhood will find him. We are scattered across this land like the dust upon the wind."

"I hope you're right," Arthur said. "But I can't help feeling that we're just wasting time."

Fasthorse sat back in his chair. "Where would you look?" he asked, waving a hand around them. "This is a big, open country, with too many places to hide. Where would you begin? You tell me."

Arthur let out a jittery breath and looked across the table. "I've come this far, haven't I?"

Fasthorse stood up and said, "Come."

Arthur followed him, coffee in hand, across the empty lower level, to a room off the outfitting shop. Fasthorse opened the door and felt for the light switch in the dark. The room lit up, Arthur stepped inside, and Fasthorse closed the door behind them. Arthur looked around the room. Canned corn over here, canned beans over there, cartons of toilet paper stacked to the ceiling in a corner.

Almost immediately, his eyes narrowed in on the two six-foot white plastic tables in the middle of the room. Positioned end to end, they held an impressive array of knives and handguns and rifles, most of which Arthur recognized. In the center was a large black compound hunting bow, with six razor-edged arrows fastened to its quiver, and its black plastic carrying case on the floor beneath it. Boxes with several choices of ammunition were stacked around each of the weapons, and at the end of one table were two sets of insulated white winter hunting suits, with two pairs of snowshoes tilted against the table's edge.

Arthur looked at Fasthorse and grinned. "What did you do, raid a Quentin Tarantino movie set?"

"I did not know what you may have brought with you, but I wanted to make sure we had every advantage."

Arthur pointed with his coffee mug at the bow. "Think you'll need that?"

Fasthorse smiled. "That little gem is the Bowtech Carbon Overdrive," he said, picking it up off the table. "It has three tensions of draw weight and can launch an arrow downrange at three hundred forty-two feet per second." He paused, letting that fact sink in, then added, "That's two hundred and thirty-three miles per hour to you desert dwellers."

"Hey, now," Arthur retorted.

Fasthorse stiffened his left arm as he pulled back on the string until it locked into place, gave Arthur a sideways glance. "The draw length is up to thirty inches, and with the binary cam system, this baby creates enough kinetic energy to take down a bull elk."

"I've always favored things that go *bang*, myself," Arthur said.

"That is because you desert dwellers do not live in the mountains where there are heavy winter snows. One shot from your rifle can bring an avalanche down on you. A bow is quiet. It kills in silence."

Fasthorse eased the tension and let the cams slowly rotate back into position, then set the bow down on the table.

"Have you ever shot a bow?"

"No," Arthur said, setting his mug of cold dregs on the plastic table.

Fasthorse grinned. "What the hell kind of Indian are you?"

"Fuck you," Arthur said politely. "The kind that can hit a fly in the ass at five hundred yards."

Fasthorse smiled. "You were always the best shooter." He walked over to a black triangular case leaning against one wall. "Why didn't you try to make sniper before we were in-country?"

Arthur thought briefly. "Because there's a difference between killing a man in a firefight and killing him from a mile away. At least he can face death with honor and hear the bullet that takes his life." Arthur paused, contemplating his next thought. "What if every man you killed, even under the flag of war, was a mark against your soul? And what if every one of those marks took away a little more from your soul until you had no soul left?"

"That is deep reflection for a man such as yourself," Fasthorse said. "And one that cannot be answered here tonight. So let's try to focus on the present, shall we?" He laid the case on the table, popped the latches, and hefted the small crossbow in his hands. "Here is what you will need. The Barrett Ghost Three-Fifty.

Only weighs about eight pounds and can fire an arrow at three hundred fifty feet per second, give or take."

Arthur looked at the contraption of strings and limbs. "Reminds me of one of the weight machines in the Border Patrol gym, except the weight machines didn't have high-powered scopes. "Think I'll stick with my three-thirty-eight Win Mag."

Fasthorse shrugged and returned the crossbow to its case. "See anything else you might like?"

"Aside from the snow-whites and the shoes," Arthur said, "not really. If this snow turns into something big, we'll need them to keep the element of surprise." He glanced down at the pistols holstered under his left arm and in his right waistband. "I've got the two Glocks. I think I'm good. And the Winchester's in the truck. All the Brotherhood needs to do is tell us where he is, and we'll do the rest."

The ring of telephones sounded from the outfitter store, the main lobby, and the desk in Fasthorse's office. The two men looked at each other and followed the sound to the phone sitting on the glass counter case. Fasthorse picked it up and answered, then listened. Then he said something in Blackfoot to the voice on the other end and hung up.

"One of the brethren found a brown Yukon and followed it to where it turned off the highway, headed into the wilderness toward a hiking trailhead. There were three people inside. He'll wait for us.

He turned to Arthur. "Let's go."

CHAPTER TWENTY-FOUR

The Yukon rolled to a stop at the far end of the snow-covered clearing. Any other time of year, this pristine landscape would be filled with the quiet beauty of snowberry and thimbleberry bushes showing off their white and red berries. Now the bushes were bare, and the tall ponderosa pines swayed heavily with their burden of new snow.

The truck's engine continued to idle in the falling snow that was already covering the tire tracks. A few windfall trees lay about the clearing, their ripped-out root systems looking as if they were trying desperately to reach through the snow and reseat themselves back in the now frozen earth. The engine stopped, and the clearing was quiet again.

"Get out," Kanesewah ordered. "We walk from here."

Gloria opened the door and climbed out, and Sharon followed suit. The blood that smeared her face was now dry. She filled her hands with snow and rubbed her face carefully, letting the pain guide her. Looking into the SUV's side window, she used a corner of blanket to dab the skin clean. Now, standing in powder that was already ankle deep, the two women watched Kanesewah slam the door and walk around to the back of the Yukon. Gloria went to join him.

Sharon stood shivering in the woolen blanket, her bruised face numb from its snow bath. An icy gust tossed the bottom of the blanket and stung her freezing face with needles of blowing snow. One fist pulled the blanket under her chin as her other hand reached behind and pulled the end over her head. Keeping her hands wrapped in the blanket, she pulled it close against her trembling body for whatever warmth it could provide. As her two captors talked in low voices at the rear of the SUV, she reconnoitered her surroundings. Trees were all she noticed—nothing but snow-covered evergreens and high mountains above them. And the only way out was the track they had taken in from the road. She chided herself for not paying attention when she had felt the truck jerk into a right turn and drop off the frosted highway before heading into the woods. Arthur's chances of finding her were getting slimmer with every minute that ticked away.

Kanesewah opened the rear hatch of the truck and pulled Gloria to him underneath it. They kissed passionately in a way that made Sharon uncomfortable. Then she heard the snap of the switchblade. She turned in time to see Kanesewah drive the knife upward into Gloria's stomach, watched her legs buckle beneath her, and saw the look of disbelief on her face. Kanesewah continued to hold her upright with the strength of one arm while he slid the blade diagonally across her belly, its angled path slicing through pancreas, colon, and small intestine. Then he moved her farther under the hatch and sat her on the edge of the cargo area.

Gloria's blood spilled freely now, coloring the snow. She sat slumped, her head hanging down and her breathing labored. Her fingers gripped the shoulders of her lover's parka, losing their strength as the last seconds of her life slipped away.

Kanesewah leaned in and whispered softly, "Let it go. Just let it go."

Gloria struggled to raise her head and said through tears, "Wh-why?"

Kanesewah glanced at Sharon, then turned back to Gloria. "Her, I need; you, I don't."

And there it was: that final, shuddering sound. He closed his eyes, reveling in the pleasure of it. Sharon watched as Gloria's last breath clouded briefly and then vanished into the falling snow. Her arms now hung motionless at her side, and her dark hair spilled from under the hood of her parka.

Sharon's panic made her immobile. Her lower lip quivered. Kanesewah ordered her to the rear of the Yukon. Was the same fate about to befall her? Was this the end? Would she be slaughtered and stuffed into the back of this truck along with Gloria and left out here in this frozen forest, to be found when the spring thaw melted the snows that had buried the truck, the snowberry bushes, and the dormant grasses?

With each reluctant step, she moved closer to Kanesewah. His expressionless stare revealed nothing as he wiped the blade of his knife on Gloria's pant leg. After smearing her blood into two long crimson stripes on the blue denim, he folded the switchblade and returned it to his coat pocket. After removing the .38 revolver from Gloria's coat pocket, he said, "Put it on." Then, looking down at her shoes, he added, "Take her boots, too.

You're about the same size. And make it fast—we need to move."

Sharon stood still, saying nothing, respecting the Navajo taboos concerning the departed.

"Don't tell me you believe in that chindi shit," Kanesewah said.

Sharon nodded slowly. "We should not be near her. I will not wear the clothes of the dead. Everything that was bad or unbalanced in her body has left, but it lingers still. I can feel it around us."

Kanesewah's eyes locked with Sharon's. "Then you'll die right here."

Sharon swallowed and began to unzip Gloria's parka, taking care not to look upon the emotionless face and staring eyes. She fought back tears as she removed the dead woman's body from the coat and laid her down in the cargo area of the truck, her legs dangling. She slipped the coat on and zipped it up, hoping the spirits that had left the body after death would not torment her.

The cold dampness of fresh blood against her belly sickened her, and she fought back the urge to vomit. Next, the boots. Gloria had changed from her cowboy boots to a pair of Sorels before they left the cottonwood grove. Sharon lifted one leg and then the other, untying and removing them as quickly as she could. She sat on the edge of the Yukon, slipped off her pumps and placed them next to Gloria's body, then tugged the boots onto her freezing feet. The Sorels were blotched with red. She shifted her feet in the snow, trying to clean them, but succeeded only in smearing them. The fleece inside felt warm, and the boots came up high enough to cover her calves. She stood and gently laid the blanket over Gloria's body as Leonard Kanesewah released the cylinder of the .38 to check the loads. He slapped it shut and tucked the gun into the front waistband of his pants before pushing past Sharon to the Yukon's cargo area. Reaching across the body, he pulled one of the duffel bags out and tossed it at her.

"Get that on," he said.

She slipped her arms through the shoulder straps and shrugged the duffel onto her back, then watched Kanesewah grab Gloria's legs and shove them carelessly into the back of the truck. He hauled out a backpack and put it on.

Sharon realized that his backpack had been filled with everything he needed for the trek. It even had a tent strapped across its top. Kanesewah had thought this through, even down to the moment of killing Gloria. But had he thought it through enough? He had not counted on Arthur tracking them.

Kanesewah thumbed the Yukon's remote and the rear hatch closed with the quiet whir of motors, sealing Sanchez's body inside. He searched the clearing before tossing the remote into the trees, where it vanished somewhere in the thickening blanket of fresh snow.

"Let's go," he said, nodding toward the third of five trailheads and stepping past her. "This way."

"Do you even know where we are?" Sharon asked, pulling up the fur-lined hood of the dead woman's parka and feeling the flakes of snow melt and trickle down her neck. Her tone was defiant. "I'm not going in there with you!"

Kanesewah stopped and turned, walked back the few feet to face her. "We're about ten miles from the Canadian border, in that direction." He pointed with a gloved hand. "I'm not going to let anyone stop me from getting there. You can either come with me or, again, you can die right here. You choose."

Sharon nodded. Kanesewah turned and moved toward the trailhead. She followed, taking care not to mix their footprints. If Arthur tracked them to the clearing, she wanted him to know that she was alive. The shoes she had left behind with Gloria's corpse would tell him that, and the dead woman's boots would give him a clear trail to follow. He would also notice that Gloria's coat was missing and would reason that Sharon had been forced to wear it. Now it was only a matter of time. The connection she had felt from the beginning was still strong between them. And, like her husband, it would never abandon her.

They walked into the woods, with the crump of their footfalls and the soft creaking of snow-laden branches the only sounds around them. With her hands deep in the pockets, Sharon pulled Gloria's coat closer to her, trying to retain what body heat she could while they walked. She wished the revolver was still in its pocket. All it would take was one shot to the back of the head—a *kill shot*, Arthur called it. But without any weapon at hand, she would have to think of some other way.

As they trudged through this mountain forest, she had seen nothing that would work even as a club. The snow was coming down thicker and faster now as the night wore on, making the slog tougher by the hour. Her lungs began to ache as the cold, thin air began to take its toll. Only the scattered tracks of squirrel and snowshoe hare could be made out crisscrossing in front of her as she shifted her mind away from her search and the exertion of plodding through the snow. Even if she were to locate something she could use, it would be impossible to pick up unless it was close enough to reach out and grab, since the crunch of the snow would betray any sort of lunging movement.

With nightfall, the temperature had begun its downward slide. Kanesewah paused periodically to look back at his trailing captive, his breath just as labored as hers. Apparently rethinking his security, he ordered her to walk in front of him so he could guide her through the maze of trees and falling snow. On his command, she led them left, then right, then straight, then right again, no doubt following the route that Kanesewah had committed to memory from the map in the car.

As the two made their way through deepening snow, the muscles of Sharon's legs throbbed with every step, and the thin mountain air continued to make each freezing breath more difficult than the last, forcing her lungs to work harder to keep her body moving. Sharon began to feel her face tighten from the cold. The snow continued to fall as if in slow motion around them, catching on her eyelashes and causing her to blink constantly. Between blinks, she searched the woods, more out of desperation than from any cognitive process. Arthur surely wouldn't be lurking anywhere close, waiting patiently for the opportunity to pounce like a cougar stalking a deer. But a predator was indeed what he had become. He was a Shadow Wolf. And outrunning any wolf was not an option. Smaller creatures would try it, but the larger, better-armed prey was apt to stand and fight. Kanesewah, Sharon knew, was not the type to run. He would stand his ground and force the outcome, whatever that might be.

"Stop," she heard him mutter behind her. "We're here."

Peering through the wafting flakes, she saw nothing at first. Then, gradually, her eyes discerned a gap in the trees, and a log cabin built long ago. Smoke rose from the stone chimney into the frozen sky. The dwelling had the look of a century-old trapper's cabin, probably built by someone searching for solitude and freedom on his own terms. The hand-squared logs were weathered gray, with patches of fresh chinking to replace whatever horsehair-and-mud filler had rotted out over the years. Two windows glowed with a warming light from the fireplace within.

"Right where I knew it would be," Kanesewah said, pushing her toward the cabin. "Don't say a word. I'll do the talking when we get close." He pulled the .38 from his waistband and slipped it into his coat pocket.

The whistling bugle of a bull elk floated in the wintry air as they stepped closer to the cabin. Kanesewah grabbed Sharon's shoulder, and they stopped walking. A shadow had moved across one window.

"Hello the cabin!" Kanesewah yelled.

No response.

"I said, hello the cabin!"

The cabin door cracked open, and a yellowish slit of angled light crossed the porch and lost itself in the snow. "I heard ya! That's far enough!" a voice yelled back. "Who are ya and whaddya want?"

A long gun barrel protruded from the slit of yellow light.

"We've been hiking up here for the last week and got caught in the snow!" Kanesewah yelled. "We saw your cabin and hoped we could maybe warm ourselves. My wife is hurt. She fell a while back and I think she broke her nose!"

More silence as the rifle barrel continued to point in their direction. The distant elk bugled again. The door moved wider, and a tall man with broad shoulders stood silhouetted in the glow. The long rifle that had been trained on them was now cradled across his chest.

"Come ahead!" the man said. "But slow, so I can see ya!"

"Remember," Kanesewah murmured, "one word out of place, and he's a dead man."

CHAPTER TWENTY-FIVE

"You and Annie ever talk about having kids?"

The question had been rolling around in Arthur's head ever since he and Abraham Fasthorse left the Three Suns main house. Now it finally spilled from his mouth as he watched the blowing snow swirl in front of the Bronco's headlights. They had just turned off the slickening blacktop of 89 onto Highway 17 and were rolling past Chief Mountain, toward Canada. Somewhere between the freezing waters of Lee Creek and the Otatso Creek Trail was a member of the Blackfoot Brotherhood who had spotted Leonard Kanesewah's Yukon disappearing into the woods.

"Sure, we talked about it," Fasthorse said. "And we tried for a solid two years. Ended up taking her to a doctor in Great Falls, and she said it wasn't Annie." He was staring out the passenger window at the dark, snow-laden forest. "That left me," he added with a sigh. "Let us just say my little swimmers are not Michael Phelps."

"I'm sorry," Arthur said. He realized at once how useless those words seemed as a method of trying to give someone solace, but they were all he had to offer.

"What about you?" Fasthorse said. "You and Sharon ever get the urge?"

Arthur took a deep breath and explained the all-too-recent past. "We talked about it again the morning she flew to Belen." He wrung the steering wheel with his hands. "I shouldn't have even hesitated like I did—shouldn't have even questioned it."

"You had no way of knowing what was to happen," Fasthorse said. "And you will have all the time in the world to make it right after we get her back."

Arthur shot him a sideways glance. "Yeah."

"We *are* going to get her back," Fasthorse reiterated. "We are Shadow Wolves. And because of this, you are my brother. That is all that needs to be said." He massaged his legs with both hands and added, "In light of day, in dark of night, no evil shall escape our sight …"

"For I am the Shadow Wolf," Arthur finished. He glanced down to Fasthorse's legs. "They must be bothering you. You sure you're up for this?"

"I am fine. Just pain brought on by the cold." He grinned. "Besides, a warrior never gives in to pain."

The highway before them churned with blowing snow. The county plows were doing what they could to keep the highway passable, but the snow seemed to be winning the first round of this bout.

Ak'is sat patiently in the back seat. He had been dividing his attention equally between the two men as they spoke, all the while keeping an eye on the approaching scene through the windshield. Suddenly, his ears perked up and his eyes fixed on a vehicle parked on the side of the road, its hazard lights flashing through the snow.

"Is that your caller?" Arthur asked.

"It is. Samuel Walking Elk and I grew up getting into trouble together. We never could keep our hands in our pockets if we were in the candy aisle. Rez police always brought us home because we were underage."

Arthur grinned and moved the Bronco in behind the flashing amber lights of a beat-up Dodge Power Wagon. He turned on his flashers and left the engine running. Both men got out as a man emerged from the idling truck and walked back to greet them.

Samuel Walking Elk was a man of average height, stocky proportions and middle-age, whose black hair fell from under his dark beaver cowboy hat and ran down over the shoulders of his fluffy red down jacket. The round face beneath the hat offered no smile, but his eyes told Arthur that he had a full grasp of the stakes involved. They met at the rear of the Dodge, then stepped away from the swirl of acrid exhaust.

"*Iiksoka'pii kitsinohsi*," Walking Elk said as he shook Fasthorse's hand.

"*Niistowa niitoyi*," Fasthorse answered before introducing Arthur. They shook hands as Fasthorse asked, "Where did they go?"

Walking Elk turned and pointed toward the opening in the tall pines across from them. "They turned in there. I drove past so they wouldn't think I was following them, and then doubled back. I've been sitting here ever since. Only turned the hazards on when the snow got bad—didn't want someone slamming into the back of me sitting here." He glanced over at the entrance again, now covered with a good fifteen inches of fresh snow and getting higher. "They haven't come out."

"Where does that lead to?" Arthur asked.

"There's a clearing about five miles in," Walking Elk said. "It's a favorite place for the adventurous white man to pretend he's one of us. A lot of hikers use it during the summer."

"How many trailheads lead from that clearing?" Fasthorse asked.

"Four that are marked, I think. The fifth trail, the middle one, leads to a mountain cabin way back in the woods somewhere. Old mountain man named Breckenridge has been living up there for the last sixty years. One of those—what do they call them—grandfathered-in people. Park Service either never wanted to make him leave, or they just figured on letting a sleeping dog lie, if you know what I mean. He's alone and likes it that way. Story is, he turned recluse after his wife died back in '81. Only comes down for supplies a few times a year on horseback, if you can believe that, dragging a pack mule just like the old days. Hibernates like a bear in the winter. You won't see him now until spring." Walking Elk looked meaningfully at them both. "He's not someone you'd want to mess with."

Arthur and Fasthorse looked at each other. Fasthorse held out his hand, and Walking Elk clasped it firmly. Arthur shook hands as well and thanked him for his help. Walking Elk nodded and walked back to the warmth of his idling truck. Sitting in the Bronco, the pair watched the Power Wagon fishtail slightly as it left the shoulder of the road, and then vanish into the falling snow. Arthur made sure the four-wheel drive was locked in and cranked the wheel hard left. The Bronco sprang across the highway and plunged its front tires deep into the snow.

The front suspension rebounded as the lugs of the wide tires bit into the terrain beneath the powder, and the Bronco set off down the single track into the woods. The ruts from the Yukon had faded considerably with the continuing snowfall, but Arthur could make out the fading trail in his headlights.

As the truck lurched and bounced along the rail, its rattling and squeaking had an almost calming effect on Arthur. Fasthorse, by contrast, just kept his eyes straight ahead.

"Maybe you should slow down, huh?" Fasthorse said.

"What?" Arthur said. "You can't be afraid of a little bumpy ride, surely. We've been bounced around way worse than this inside an APC."

"Yes! But you were not driving it!"

Almost four miles in, the woods opened up, and the pair could see a clearing with several blowdown tamaracks and pines. At the far end, under a mounting blanket of snow, was the brown GMC Yukon. Arthur kept his foot down and bulled across the opening. Slamming the brake to the floor, he slid the Bronco to a stop just right of the truck. Arthur jumped out with one of the Glocks in his hand. Fasthorse piled out the other side in a crouch, his 1911 Colt .45 out and up in both hands while his eyes scanned for any movement in the surrounding trees. Seeing no one, he moved fast around the Bronco to the rear hatch of the Yukon. Arthur was staring through the smoked rear glass, at the body of Gloria Sanchez.

"Kanesewah killed her," Fasthorse said.

"Probably didn't need her anymore," Arthur replied.

Fasthorse scanned the truck's cargo area. "Looks like Sharon took her coat and boots."

"Or Kanesewah made her put them on." Arthur pointed through the glass. "Those are her shoes. He's taken her with him because he knows I'm following him." "The tracks are still visible," Fasthorse said, nodding at the series of dips heading uphill in the snow. "It cannot have been long since they went into the woods. We must move now, or the snow will cover them completely and wipe out our chance of finding them."

Arthur returned the Glock to his shoulder holster as he walked to the open door of the Bronco. Leaning in, he hit the switch on the dash and dropped the rear glass. Fasthorse opened the tailgate, and Ak'is bounded over the back seat and out into the snow. He turned about and stood looking at them, his hot breath fogging in front of him. Shaking the snow from his head, he put his nose to work in the air. Arthur flung back the machine-made blanket and pulled the .338 Magnum rifle from its sheath. Fasthorse grabbed the two snow suits from a duffel, handed Arthur one, and they zipped in.

"I also packed these in case we have to separate," he said and held up two pairs of headsets.

"Two-ways?" Arthur smiled.

"Just stick it on your head in case we have to split up to take out this asshole." Fasthorse slipped the harness on and adjusted it, then pulled the white hood over his head. Arthur followed suit. "Just like back in the day," Fasthorse told him. "They automatically link up when you turn them on, and we're good to go. PTT, like always."

Arthur hit the push-to-talk button. "Roger that."

"Snow's getting deeper." Fasthorse was looking up the trail. "It will be deeper the farther in we go. Let's strap in."

Arthur dug the snowshoes from under the remaining duffels. After they strapped them on, he stuffed a box of rifle cartridges into a coat pocket and did the same with a box of Glock rounds. Fasthorse took the compound bow from its case, checked the graphite shafts mounted to its side, and said, "Let's go."

Arthur paused and pointed at the arrows. "Don't you want to take any more?"

Fasthorse grinned. "I do not need even this many."

CHAPTER TWENTY-SIX

The cabin was filled with the smoky scent of burning tamarack wood, and the warmth spilling from the hearth welcomed them as they entered. The old man stood with his rifle at his side and let them pass. He had a rough salt-and-pepper beard and looked to Sharon to be a lean 250 pounds. With a wave of his hand, the old man offered them seats at the small pine table that stood a safe distance from the fireplace. She took note of the snowshoes that decorated one wall, and the cast-iron pots and skillets hanging from a low log beam. Kanesewah shrugged out of his backpack as Sharon slid the large duffel off her shoulder, and they left both on the floor by the table. Sharon said nothing as she took off Gloria's parka and draped it over the back of a chair.

"Damn, young-'un," the old man said, "you did take a tumble. My name's Breckenridge. John Henry Breckenridge." He leaned the rifle against the wall by the potbelly stove. "I've got a first-aid kit around here somewheres."

While he rummaged through an old camelback trunk,

Sharon continued to take in her surroundings: the fireplace built of local rock, the squared logs hand-hewn by a craftsman long dead, the rough plank flooring, the pine-board table and worn wooden chairs, the kerosene lamp that cast their shadows onto bare log walls. From the blue enamelware coffeepot on the potbelly, her eyes followed the stove's flue up to where it angled into the wall, just below the roof beam.

"Got it!" the old man said, holding up the white plastic box with the red cross. Closing the trunk, he set the kit on the table. Then he pumped a pot of water and set it on the potbelly to heat. "Soon's 'at heats up, you can tend to your wife."

He wandered back over where the rifle leaned against the wall. "So, you two got caught in the storm, eh? Mighty careless, don'tcha think?" He picked up the enamelware coffeepot from the stove and asked him if they could use some. "Made it fresh a little while ago."

"Thank you," Kanesewah said. "We must have gotten caught up in all the natural beauty of this area. And our weather radio doesn't seem to work up here."

* * *

Kanesewah could see through the open door to the bedroom at the end of the cabin, and the old brass bed that took up half the space. It must have gleamed at one time, but now it stood empty and tarnished. The old man must have some rope around here somewhere for hanging and dressing a deer. He pictured stripping Sharon naked and tying her wrists to the thick, tarnished posts at the head, and her ankles to the posts at the foot, her legs spread wide and inviting. He imagined standing at the end of the bed and looking down at her openness to him, studying it, watching it glisten as her breasts heaved and her belly undulated with fear. And then he would play with her, just as he had with the Braun girl and so many others. And out here, there would be no one to hear her screams. No one to disrupt his entertainment. All he had to do was rid himself of the old man.

* * *

"My wife had me haul that thing up here," Breckenridge said, noticing his guest's interest in the brass bed. "Damn pain in the ass, but she wanted some kind of civilization up here, so I compromised."

"Don't we all," Kanesewah remarked. "Coffee smells good."

"Don't get any visitors up here," Breckenridge said. "Sorry 'bout the rifle, but you can't be too careful."

"No harm," Kanesewah said. "It's understandable—all kinds of weird people in this world."

Breckenridge finished pouring coffee into three chipped enamelware cups and set the pot back on the stove. He brought two cups to his guests. "Got no cream. Take mine black as sin with a little sugar tossed in." From a wooden shelf just right of the stove, he took a white glass sugar bowl resembling a white basket with a nesting hen as the lid. "My wife got this when we moved up here forty-five years back." He spooned three mounds of sugar into his cup, stirred vigorously, and put the chicken back on the nest. "You want some?"

Sharon shot a quick look at Kanesewah and said, "Yes. Thank you."

Breckenridge placed the bowl on the table, handed them each a paper napkin, and walked back over by the rifle, as if to check on the pot of water. It had started to steam, so he picked it up with a pot holder and set it on a clay tile on the table.

Kanesewah was playing along with the charade and reached for the cloth, but Sharon snatched it up and said she would take care of it. He gave her a stern look that the old man seemed to notice over the top of his coffee cup.

"How long did you say you been hikin' around?" Breckenridge asked between sips.

Kanesewah spooned in two mounds of sugar and stirred. "About two weeks, right, hon?"

Sharon looked at him. "Right," she answered, gently pressing the hot, wet rag against her face and letting the warm water soothe her bruised and swollen cheek and nose. "About two weeks, I'd guess. It's so beautiful up here, we kind of lost track."

"Can't disagree with you there," Breckenridge said. "The wife and I knew this was the place for us the minute we got out here." He looked at Kanesewah. "Good thing you got a woman likes the outdoors. Most of 'em's version of roughing it is a motel somewhere with no room service, if you can even get 'em out here at all."

As the old man opened the potbelly's door to throw in a couple of splits, Sharon watched Kanesewah take note of the carving-knife block on the wall table, and a worn leather holster with what looked like a large caliber revolver dangling from a wooden peg by the door … and, of course, the rifle leaning against the wall.

"I know a lot of the Blackfoot around here," Breckenridge said, "but you two don't look familiar to me."

"We're not from around here," Kanesewah answered. "We're up from New Mexico on our honeymoon." He made no mention of any tribal affiliation.

Breckenridge grinned widely. "Ain't that somethin'. Congratulations!" He toasted with his cup and took a drink of coffee. "Pity you're stuck here with me. I remember bein' newlyweds, with only one thing on our mind."

Sharon glanced at Kanesewah, then at Breckenridge, and managed to give a self-conscious smile. Then she dipped the now-reddish rag into the hot water and wrung it out. All she could think about was how to keep this old man alive. She resumed cleaning her tender face as the water began to turn the color of pink lemonade.

"No need to be embarrassed, ma'am," Breckenridge said. "When you get to be my age, sometimes you just spout off without thinkin'." His eyes turned to Kanesewah. "Apologies to you and your bride."

Kanesewah sipped his coffee and smiled. No offense had been taken. Sharon moved the warm cloth over her forehead and down her other cheek, then scrubbed the dried blood trickle from her throat. she rinsed the rag and wrung it out tightly. The water now had the hue of strawberry Jell-O.

"Pretty as a picture, ma'am," Breckenridge said.

Sharon smiled and laid the rinsed and wrung cloth on the tabletop. Breckenridge picked up both pot and cloth and, opening the front door, tossed the water into the snowy night. After closing the door, he walked back over to the stove and tossed the cloth onto the wall table, by the knife block. Sharon drank some of her coffee and patted her lips with the napkin—a move that surreptitiously drew Breckenridge's attention. She had held the napkin in her left hand, and the diamond wedding ring was hard to miss. The next time Kanesewah's beefy left hand lifted his coffee cup to his lips, it was obvious that he wore no ring of any kind.

* * *

The old man's eyes went down casually, as if he had seen nothing of note. But he had seen it. These two had been trying damned hard to seem at ease, but they had an edginess that just didn't feel like a couple of randy newlyweds. They appeared tense and uneasy. The man was keeping his cool, though; he would give him that. But he always seemed to be thinking. Breckenridge could see the wheels turning inside that busy mind. The woman, on the other hand, wasn't very good at hiding her agitation. Yes, sir, something was damned odd about this pair. He would have to tread lightly with them. And for right now, he wasn't going to stray any farther than an arm's length from his rifle.

"You two hungry?" he said. The fireplace continued to pop.

* * *

"We could eat something, sure, but we don't want to put you out," Kanesewah said. He despised this idle conversation bullshit. The faster this old man shut up, the better.

"Hell, you ain't puttin' nobody out. Be glad to fix you up something. Ain't gonna be fancy, but it'll be good." Setting his blue cup on the edge of the stove to keep it warm, he pulled aside a muslin curtain and looked through the canned goods on the pantry shelves. "I stocked up for winter with a lot of beans and vegetables and stuff like that. Got a bunch of soups, too—like this beef and potato here. Couple cans of that'll stick to your ribs. Sound good?"

Kanesewah eyed the knife block below the canned goods and mixes. He had the switchblade in his coat pocket, but one of the larger carving knives would make shorter work of it in case the woman decided to get brave. And then there was the rifle. If he made a grab for it, could he beat the old man to it? The geezer was big and looked strong as a mule. And the woman—did she have enough strength left to help the old man try to stop him from getting to either weapon? Who the fuck knew. Either way, this was going to be fun.

"Beef and potato sounds great," Kanesewah said, and shot a sideways glance at Sharon, sitting with her warm blue cup of coffee in both hands. "That okay, honey?"

* * *

Sharon nodded tentatively.

"You have bears up here, right?" Kanesewah said. "We thought we saw one yesterday."

Breckenridge took a pot from the beam and a can opener

from a shelf by the stove and turned. "That so?" he said. He opened both cans with quick turns of his wrist and tossed the opener back onto the shelf. After using a spoon to lift the sharp-edged lids, he pushed them back with his fingers. "Well, most bears—and we got both kinds in these parts: grizzlies and black—start hibernatin' 'bout this time. So, if you seen one, it was headin' for a den and won't be out again till April." He scooped the contents of both soup cans into the pot. "You ever hear of a guy named Treadwell?" Breckenridge asked.

Kanesewah and Sharon shook their heads.

"He was what you'd call a real bear lover. Spent thirteen years up in Alaska at a place they call the Grizzly Maze, trackin' 'em, filmin' 'em, and livin' with 'em. Some say he wasn't firin' on all cylinders, but who the hell knows. Now, I been around these bears up here since 1970 and I wouldn't trust 'em any futher'n I could toss one. They're wild and unpredictable; I don't care what anybody says. But this guy trusted 'em *too* much. And sure enough, a big grizz came into his camp one night and killed him and the woman he was with. Ate 'em, too." Breckenridge shook his head over the pot of bubbling soup. "I heard the audio once. He was always video-recordin' shit. Ghastly, hearin' a man get killed by a grizz." He absently stirred the soup. "It just rips and tears at you while you scream, never payin' you no mind. 'Cause it don't care. It's just doing what nature taught a grizz to do." He turned and looked at his guests. "You're just part of the food supply."

Sharon drank the last of her coffee and asked for more. Breckenridge pulled the pot off the stove and filled her cup, then motioned toward Kanesewah, who nodded and held out his cup.

While his guests sugared to their coffee, he filled a couple of blue enamelware bowls with hot soup and set them on the table. Then he puttered about while the two ate, never straying too far from the rifle.

Sharon took a tantalizing spoonful and blew on it, glancing over her spoon at Kanesewah. He was shoveling the soup into his mouth, with his left arm curled around the bowl as if he were afraid she might steal it. She spooned the soup into her mouth and reveled in its steamy goodness. The thick, savory broth tasted like heaven, and it felt good going down her throat.

She had caught Breckenridge also paying attention to Kanesewah's table manners. Men who had spent time behind bars ate that way, protecting their meal from fellow inmates wanting to assert their dominance in the dog-eat-dog world of prison. It was a habit that persisted, even in life outside the walls.

"You're not eating?" Sharon asked after her third spoonful of the meaty stew.

"No, ma'am," Breckenridge said, "I ate earlier. Seems like you two are hungry, though. Glad to see it." Catching her eye for a split instant while Kanesewah looked down to scoop up another bite, he said, "You let me know if you want some more. Two of them cans make a lot." Kanesewah, with his head down, missed Breckenridge's knowing wink to Sharon.

Sharon missed nothing. She spooned some more soup as the old man's eyes slid in the direction of the rifle, then to the .45 holstered on the peg by the door. Sharon slowly shook her head while stirring the soup in her bowl. Kanesewah continued scarfing away, his spoon clattering against the enameled metal bowl. When there was nothing left to scrape up, he said, "Think

I'll have some more, if you don't mind." He stood up. "That is some good stuff."

Sharon watched Kanesewah cross over to the stove, take the wooden spoon, and ladle more soup into his bowl. Her eyes crossed back to the old man, and she nodded. *Grab the rifle!*

He hesitated, and the moment was gone. Instead of the wooden spoon, Kanesewah held a carving knife. An eyeblink later, it was hilt deep in Breckenridge's belly. The coffee cup clattered on the plank floor as the old man's hands found Kanesewah's throat and clamped tightly around it. As the wide blade twisted through the old man's insides, his strength quickly waned. Kanesewah shoved him away and watched him stumble toward the rifle before falling to the floor.

Sharon fell from her chair to her knees beside him and pressed both hands to the wound.

"Hold on, John Henry." She turned her head to look up at Kanesewah, who was now standing over them, the carving knife dripping on the wooden floor. "You bastard!"

She gazed down into Breckenridge's fading eyes and felt his breath grow weak and shallow. She looked up once more at Kanesewah's emotionless stare, then solemnly closed John Henry Breckenridge's dead eyes with her palm.

"You in the cabin!" a voice yelled. "I know you're in there, Kanesewah! Let her go and we'll talk!"

Leonard Kanesewah darted to a curtained window and pushed it slightly aside with his left hand while his right hand still held the carving knife. The forest was dark, and the moon was hidden behind a bank of clouds.

Hearing Arthur's voice, Sharon felt hope wash over her. She

had always known he would find her, because she never lost the feeling of connection. She sprang up from the floor and grabbed the worn towel from the washstand where it hung.

Kanesewah darted from the window and grabbed her by the arm, jerking her around to face him. "That your husband out there?"

"Damn right," she snarled. "And now you're going to die."

Kanesewah grinned and grunted a short laugh. "You first."

CHAPTER TWENTY-SEVEN

Arthur Nakai and Abraham Fasthorse crouched behind the large trunk of a fallen tree some thirty yards from the cabin. Ak'is stood at attention behind them, ears perked, nose twitching, golden eyes piercing the night.

The snow had all but stopped, and the wind had died down to barely a breeze. But at 9,500 feet, the cold still managed to penetrate Arthur's clothing in its ongoing campaign to freeze the marrow of his bones. Only the adrenaline coursing through his veins was keeping the pain at bay. And Abraham, with his aging wounds, was no doubt feeling it far more. But the Blackfoot lived here; he was used to this weather. And like Arthur, he had been well trained to tolerate pain during his three tours in such places as Kabul and Kandahar.

"You suppose the old man is in there with them?" Arthur asked as his breath fogged in front of him.

"I would bet on it," Fasthorse replied. "Unless Kanesewah has already killed him to remove his last barrier to freedom.

Less than ten miles of valley is all that stands between him and Canada."

"You're forgetting the two of us," Arthur pointed out.

Fasthorse nodded in agreement. "How do you want to play this?"

Arthur peered over the fallen trunk carefully enough to study the terrain. They were about forty-five degrees right of the cabin's front door, ninety feet away with no obstructions. Flanking the door were two newer double-hung, simulated multipaned windows. The logs of the right wall were unbroken with windows of any kind, and he had already checked the left and back walls. Like every century-old cabin he had ever seen, this one had no back door. This put Sharon in even greater danger because they lost the element of surprise. Arthur glanced up. A gibbous moon rode high behind dense clouds that floated in the night sky as if they had been conjured by the father of the sun god himself. Tklehanoai was carrying the moon on his back this night and seemed to be on his side. Arthur looked left to a stretch of higher ground near seven o'clock, just past the edge of the clearing, and began plotting a line of fire.

"That high ground at seven o'clock," he said. "Think you can get a clean shot from there if I can get him outside?"

"It looks a little farther away than here," Fasthorse said, "but there are no obstructions that I can see, so yes. Turn on the PTT now." He put out his hand. Arthur took it. "This is almost over, my friend. But remember, the fire burns hot in your heart. Do not let its smoke blind your eyes."

Arthur gave a brief nod, and Fasthorse took off at a fast jog through the snow-laden trees, his snowshoes kicking up little puffs of white as he made his way through the woods. Arthur switched on his radio. Ak'is watched Fasthorse vanish from sight, then moved up into position beside Arthur. The canine's breathing remained steady and even, which was more than Arthur could say for himself. Everything he had done, witnessed, or even thought in the past few days had come down to this moment, this place. Now. Arthur watched as the curtains in the window left of the front door fell together, cutting off the yellowish glow that had escaped from them. Then the window to the right of the door went dark. Arthur looked left, searching for Fasthorse, but could not see him. He pressed the push-to-talk button on his radio. "You in position?"

Static. "I am ready."

Again Arthur shouted, "Kanesewah! Let her go and we'll talk! Nobody has to get hurt!"

* * *

Leonard Kanesewah glanced sideways at Sharon as he picked up the old man's rifle and worked the bolt. Seeing the loaded cartridge, he pushed it back into the chamber and walked back to the front door. He opened it a few inches and braced it with his right foot.

"You think this is some movie, Husband?" he shouted back. "There is nothing to talk about! I have your wife, and you're going to let me go. Then maybe I will give her back to you! If you don't, then she will die, and it will be because of you!"

"I can't let you leave the cabin with her!" Arthur shouted. "This is where it ends!"

Kanesewah glanced at the revolver hanging in its holster from the wooden peg beside him. "It amazes me how you play with your wife's life! I would have thought she meant more to you than that!"

* * *

Abraham Fasthorse held his position in the trees. After getting to his vantage point and settling into position, he had replaced the warm glove on his right hand with a shooting glove, which left his fingers free to feel the cold. He wrapped his left forearm with his leather bracer, removing any possibility of the bulky winter camo interfering with his arrow's flight. His breathing was calm and relaxed, his heartbeat steady, as he listened to the shouted conversation. As far as Kanesewah knew, only Arthur stood in his way.

"She does!" Arthur replied. "That's why this is where you will die!"

Kanesewah pulled the revolver from its holster and stuck it in the front waistband of his pants.

"I have to hand it to you, Husband!" Kanesewah shouted. "I underestimated you! You are a worthy enemy. It's a shame I will have to kill you!"

Sharon remained still, crouched on the floor near the old man's body. Her eyes roamed the cabin for anything that would distract him long enough to let her break free and get safely across the snow to Arthur. Getting to the knife block was impossible, which left the coffeepot or the remaining soup sitting on the woodstove: both hot and able to deliver second-degree burns on contact. The lamp on the table was close at hand, too. She could grab it and toss it in the hope of breaking it by Kanesewah and covering him in burning kerosene. But if she missed, he would surely put a bullet in her, and her only hope then would be to die quickly, before fire consumed the cabin. Whatever course of action she chose, she would have to work fast and make every move count.

"Let my wife go and you don't have to die tonight!" Arthur yelled.

"You don't understand, Husband! I'm in no mood to bargain, and only one of us is going to die tonight!" Kanesewah glanced back at the woman crouched meekly on the floor, then returned his attention to the cracked door, held open by his foot. "What is it our ancestors used to say? 'It is a good day to die!'"

Sharon sprang toward the stove. With the towel wrapped around her hand, she grabbed the handle of the bubbling pot and charged toward Kanesewah. He spun as she swung the pot with all the force she could muster. The scalding soup brought an agonizing scream as it plastered his face, causing him to stagger back from the door, waving his arms frantically in front of him. Dropping the rifle to the floor, he swiped at his burning face with one hand while he pulled the .45 from his waistband with the other. "You fucking bitch!" Shots rang out in the cabin, the bullets missing the kerosene lamp and slamming into the hundred-year-old log walls.

* * *

Outside, the gunshots echoed in the clear mountain air. Fasthorse quickly wrapped the strap on his Foldback release around his right wrist and buckled it. He pulled an arrow from the quiver on his bow, nocked it to the string, and held it with the index finger of his left hand while he flicked his right wrist and let the Foldback fly forward. Then, fitting the small hook of the release into the loop on his string, he drew the bow and felt the cams lock into position at the anchor point at the end of his pull. His left arm was steady, and his draw hand was positioned just below his right ear. He could smell the beeswax on the bowstring pressing against his right nostril. His index finger rested at the ready, on top of the release's small trigger. He slowed his breathing and leveled his shot.

"Come on," he whispered. "Show your ugly face."

* * *

The gunfire from the cabin ended abruptly. Though Sharon could hear little above the ringing in her ears, she saw the Colt's slide stick in the open position. This was her chance. Until Kanesewah could replace the magazine, he was out of rounds.

Quietly as she could, she darted around him as he thumbed the pistol's release. She saw the empty magazine bounce lightly on the floor as she made a run for the door. She barged out the door and down the porch steps, into the deep snow. Kanesewah came charging out the cabin door after her, firing blindly as he ran across the porch.

Post-holing frantically through the snow, Sharon put four, five, six steps between herself and the pursuing terror before something grabbed her right wrist and jerked her violently backward, reeling her hard against its heaving chest. An arm clasped her torso with all the strength of a hydraulic vise.

* * *

Fasthorse felt the urge to let fly rising steadily within him and resisted it. Arthur had stood as soon as the door opened, resting the .338 on the tree trunk. He acquired his target and put it in the crosshairs, but one thing prevented both men from firing: Sharon's body had now become her captor's shield.

* * *

Ak'is made a low, guttural growl. The sound, resonating from somewhere deep within the animal, was unlike any that Arthur had heard before. He glanced down to where the animal had been standing, and looked up just in time to see him vanish into the woods on his right. "Good boy," he said softly. He looked back down the scope at Kanesewah and Sharon, standing in front of the log cabin, backlit in the open doorway.

Kanesewah held the muzzle of a large pistol pressed firmly against Sharon's head. "I am not afraid to die, Husband!" he yelled. "But I know *she* is! Now, come out and show yourself so we can end this!"

Arthur heard Sharon sneer, "I thought you never used a gun. Guns are for cowards, remember?"

Kanesewah pressed the muzzle harder into the soft spot behind her right ear, forcing her head to the left. "Shut up!" he growled. His eyes never left the woods. "Come on, Husband! Show yourself, or I swear I will pull this trigger and you can watch me splatter her brains in the snow!"

* * *

Abraham Fasthorse continued his slow, even breathing, keeping his sight eye still, ready for the fleeting instant when he would pull the trigger and let his arrow fly. He watched as Arthur lowered the .338, resting the buttstock in the snow and the barrel against the snow-covered tree trunk. Watched him take off his PTT harness and step slowly around the tree's massive base, the snow crunching beneath his feet.

"Here I am," he said, arms outstretched at his side, palms toward the sky. "Let her go."

"NO!" Sharon cried.

Kanesewah jerked her back against him. "The dutiful husband," he said. "The knight in armor willing to sacrifice his own life for his woman's." He tilted his head as if witnessing some curious animal behavior, then pulled the gun barrel away from Sharon's head and leveled it at Arthur. "Touching, but I think I will put a bullet in you anyway and let you watch as I enjoy your woman!"

Arthur continued to step slowly forward, arms still outstretched at his sides. Fasthorse waited. His left arm was beginning to tire, but the stakes had just gone up, and he breathed new life into the muscle fatigue.

His eyes caught movement off to the right as Ak'is materialized at the edge of the darkened forest. An eerie growl rumbled up from his chest and through his bared teeth and fogged the cold air in front of him. The wolf-dog's ears were laid back against his head, and his hackles stood on end. Fasthorse quickly returned his eye to the peep sight on the bowstring.

Kanesewah turned, distracted by the animal. "Call off the wolf!" he yelled. "Call it off, or she's dead!"

Abraham Fasthorse knew that this was likely to be his only moment. At this distance, he had just two options: the right eye socket or the right temple—the only spots where an arrow could easily penetrate the human skull. Kanesewah's instant of distraction by the wolf-dog gave Fasthorse the third of a second needed for the arrow to cross the thirty yards that separated them.

He saw the fletching disappear into the shallow skin of the right temple. He imagined the three razor edges slicing through the medial lobe and the amygdala before emerging out the left side, just in front of the left ear. Kanesewah never knew that anything at all had happened. He simply ceased to exist.

* * *

Sharon felt the warm spatter against the back of her neck and left ear, then felt the arm around her torso relax and drop. His body listed right; then the knees collapsed and it crumpled into the deep snow. The revolver sank into the powder at Sharon's feet, leaving a gun-shaped impression.

She saw Arthur bounding toward her, his snowshoes throwing up a small blizzard behind him. And she felt his arms surround her, his lips kissing hers ever so softly. Her legs buckled beneath her, and they sank into the snow together as she felt herself dissolve into great, heaving sobs.

Abraham Fasthorse stepped out of the darkness, bow at his side, and made his way to them. He placed his hand on Arthur's right shoulder and breathed a sigh of exhausted relief as Sharon looked up at him. He smiled back softly and said nothing.

Ak'is pressed himself against her and nuzzled her face, the warm tongue licking the salty tears from her cheeks. She managed to wrap an arm around the huge head and pull it close, feeding on its warmth and burying her face in the thick fur.

Arthur kissed the top of her head and said softly, "And you said he was just *my* dog."

ACKNOWLEDGMENTS

I am deeply and forever grateful to Richard Curtis, agent extraordinaire, who took a chance and believed in my work and my future. Thanks also to Mystery Writers of America and Kier Graff for their guidance while I struggled in the land of the unknowns. And to Jeffrey Yamaguchi, Lauren Maturo, and Gregory Boguslawski of Blackstone Publishing for their enthusiastic welcome into the fold. And, of course, my tremendous thanks to Michael J. Carr, my editor and true north, for helping me give my dream wings.